BLOOD
BORDER

by

M.H. VESSEUR

BLOOD BORDER

A Radio Detective

A novel by
M.H. Vesseur

Vibes Publishing

Copyright © 2016 M.H. Vesseur

Published by Vibes
www.mhvesseur.com
www.facebook.com/MHVesseur

Second edition
ISBN 978-94-91908-32-3 (paperback, 2nd edition)
ISBN 978-94-91908-03-3 (epub with DRM)
ISBN 978-94-91908-33-0 (epub with DRM for Apple iBooks
and Kobo)

Blood Border

One

The door got out of the way. It was as simple, and violent, as that.

The Rodriguez family was incomplete when the gang members made their entrance. Ramon, the father, had not yet returned from his work in the rubber factory. Perhaps the perpetrators knew this, but that was highly unlikely. Street gang violence had been rampant in the slum for a long time now. These young men knew no fear and today they were after the eldest Rodriguez's daughter, Carolina. She was only thirteen, but in their eyes she was old enough for practically anything they could think of.

Neighbors had been warning the family about this. Other citizens of the slums had sent their young daughters, and sons for that matter, away on the long journey across the border to the relative safety and wealth of one of the neighboring countries. But these journeys were risky and expensive, and Ramon Rodriguez in particular had not felt like giving up yet. "We can not all abandon our country," he used to say. "It's the wrong way to go. We must take a stand and fight this violence."

But when they finally arrived, kicking in the front door of the family's shack built of wood, cardboard and a roof of corrugated iron, Ramon was not at home, which left his wife and children to face their adversaries alone.

And a pretty sight it was not.

"You're coming with us," said one of the gang boys, pointing at young Carolina.

He was slim, all muscle and athletic limbs and tattoos and scars — and in that utterly identical to his comrades. Their hair was over their ears and greasy, and they were grinning smiles like piano keyboards. The boy who did the talking was bare from the waist up, looking as if he came from the beach on a hot summer night. As if nothing out of the ordinary was going on.

But the gang boys had not counted on the attitude of the women of the house. Imbued with a strong sense of self-assurance, given to them through the years by their father and husband Ramon, they lurked forward without giving it another thought. Six children and an adult, overweight woman could muster quite a force.

"Kill the bitches!" the leader screamed before one of his stand-alone teeth was kicked out of his mouth and two girls grabbed his knife and gun from his belt.

By then, the boy next to him had been relocated to a horizontal position underneath the mother, who possessed no fighting skill worth mentioning but did pretty good anyway by throwing her considerable weight up and down.

Within moments, everybody was on the floor, but it didn't last long. The gang boys were a lot stronger, and before long they were back on their feet with Carolina between them, and they walked back to the door, pointing their guns at the woman and the girls on the floor.

"That's the last time you refused to obey our law," said the leader. "You are all going to die and you" — he looked at Carolina — "are going to be mine. And I will share you with all my brothers too. You should be proud. You will be the one who will do all the learning for your entire family."

They laughed and cocked their guns.

Everybody was screaming. Carolina was trying to free herself from the boys' grips but she couldn't.

Then a dark shadow hurled from the outside and smashed into them with incredible force.

"Father!" screamed one of the girls.

Compared to the gang boys, Ramon Rodriguez was a small man. His factory clothes were torn and dusty and were hanging from his thin shoulders as if he had shrunk since buying them. His bald head was shining with sweat. But he was built strong, like a tiny bull. He had brought a piece of wood with him and he attacked them with force and speed. Before the gang boys were able to react, they were already severely hurt. Blood and teeth were flying from them. Two guns were on the floor. Ramon grabbed the third to make sure the bullets were fired into the roof instead of his family.

Ramon hit the leader in the face and continued hitting until the other two grabbed their fellow member by the arms and disappeared from the shack.

While his wife and children rushed to him, a thousand thoughts ran through Ramon's mind. He watched the dark wound on Carolina's forehead, the blood dripping beside her eye, and her torn dress.

This is it, he thought. Can't fight it no more. They will be back tomorrow with more. It's like they told me: once they want your daughter, they'll take her and there ain't no mountain high enough to hide on when that happens.

While his wife touched his bloody forehead with a wet cloth, he let the truth of that sink in. And it felt like a relief. It really did. Because after all the years of watching his country sink into that dark gang land, where thugs ruled and no one could do anything about it and the government corruption opened all the gates of hell, after all the waiting without much hope, he now saw a light.

"I'm going to bring you all to safety," he said, spreading his arms and hugging some of his children.

He suddenly felt confident. So many families had left before them; the road to the free world was already cut through the land.

And paved with gold. Hadn't the president of one of these countries said that all immigrants were welcome?

Two

The police helicopter made its expected round at 10.30 PM above the series of skyscrapers in the city's financial district. It approached across the river, ascended quickly to reach roof level and then hovered above the buildings, its cameras spying on the streets below. It was gone in the distance in a matter of minutes.

As soon as it was out of sight, something stirred on top of a dark building. Most of the offices here were brightly lit. Some from the inside, where cleaners were busy on their late night shifts, or where management teams were arguing during meetings that had gone on for too long, or where employees were busy studying the markets on the other side of the world through their monitors. Other buildings were lit from the outside, their chromium plating mirroring the city lights.

But not this building. Except for some warm lights from the street level entrance, a large lobby with teak on the walls and dark tropical plants abundant, its eighty floors were dark. Its windows seemed to reflect nothing.

On the roof, dark figures moved. They unfolded equipment in the vague light of the moon; large hang-gliders. The metal flashed in the night and if there had been anyone around, they might have noticed the automatic weapons attached to the backs of these men, dressed in black ninja-like outfits and their faces covered partially with black cloth.

Within minutes after the disappearance of the helicopter, they jumped off the top of the building. As three winged shadows they flew between the skyscrapers, gaining height as they went. While they climbed, they kept in the city shades as much as they could. Slowly they moved towards one of the buildings a few blocks away. The one with the huge sign on it: *WCBN Radio - Home of the Bizz Jockey.*

They rushed upwards and "landed" on the side of the building. They didn't touch down, they just lifted their wings in a daring back flip and then held on to the glass with special equipment: bellows shaped apparatus that sucked a vacuum against the glass. While they were hanging on the building's facade, one of them cut a circular hole in the glass, pushed it in. Within moments, all three of them had disappeared into the building, folding their wings away like giant bats.

Everything was dark up there. Many floors down, on the broadcasting floors, the building radiated bright lights.

===

Job Messner woke up from a light sleep, his face on the keyboard of his laptop, his arms slammed on the table in front of him, one of his arms soaked with the coffee he had apparently spilled when he fell asleep.

He sometimes retreated to one of the higher floors of the WCBN Radio building to concentrate on impromptu lines he had to come up with for the business talk radio show The Boardroom. His boss, talk show host Carl Pappas, was also known as the Bizz Jockey, a big-mouthed disc jockey who had a worldwide audience of at least ten million business people. From secretary to CEO, they all tuned in to his show regularly, and they did that with beating hearts. They loved and feared Carl Pappas at the same time, for his honesty and his spontaneous way of dealing with worldwide business issues. He could scold at the world's largest corporation and then carry on and tell a joke. Many of the lines spoken by Pappas were basically written by Messner.

No one would find Job Messner here, in one of the offices that was usually abandoned after five in the afternoon. He loved to go up here, dim the lights and work on some great lines for his boss.

Nobel Prize stuff, he always said while he worked in the dark.

Nobel stuff or not, never did he fall asleep, never did he wet himself with coffee. Being the head writer for the show, the one who came up with important monologues and jokes and a lot more, he felt he was too important to miss even an instant of duty.

When Job lifted his head, the screen of his laptop lit up again and with one eye he saw that the radio broadcast was yet to begin.

He sighed with relief, but it was a short sigh. Suddenly he realized that he had been woken by a loud thud. He turned, but before he saw anything he was dealt a decisive blow by a rifle butt.

The remaining light faded from his consciousness.

Three

On his console on the other side of one of the studio's windows, sound engineer Don Wozniak pressed a button. Above and around Carl Pappas, the bizz jockey, the lights dimmed, creating the proper ambiance for tonight's guests. Through years of experience, Pappas had developed a feel for what was needed to have his guests say more on live radio than they intended. More than they had ever felt possible. It was a subtle combination of arguments, smooth talking, pressure from other people at the radio table or on the phone, music and, last but not least, temperature, humidity and lighting. All of this was to some extend orchestrated with the guest and the topic in mind.

Carl Pappas smiled at his sound engineer. He felt good about tonight's program. The topic was important for it had a political component. Basically, Pappas' show The Boardroom was all about business, but tonight it had an edge. He was going the extra mile.

The dimming of the lights also meant that Hitomi Sakamoto, his producer, was about to enter the radio room to bring in his guest for the show.

"Listen, Carl," said Don through the speaker system, his voice mixed through the finest technology to make it sound much deeper and more mysterious than in real life — a little practical joke he liked to play. "Wasn't Job supposed to come in last minute to bring you some of his Nobel Prize winning new lines?"

"He did say he was going up," said Carl. "But it was stuff for the second half. So he's probably not ready yet. Besides, we have ten more minutes."

"Whatever you say, boss, but Job Messner is not one to be late. He said he'd be back before we go live. That's what he said."

"I'm sure he did, Don," said Carl, turning his attention to his papers again.

The sound engineer was a beefy man in his early thirties, a tech wizard who had a natural way of being cool under all kinds of pressures, including that of peers. Peanut bags lay around his console, empty cups of coffee and snack wrappers. Piles of papers from the editorial staff concerning audio requirements during the show. His room smelled of nicotine, which he smoked on the roof now and then, albeit illegally. Above his unshaven jaw his glasses, thick, black, rectangular, and large, and his black, greased hair, standing up in arrows pointing in several directions gave him a Saturday morning TV cartoon appearance. He had the looks of a man you'd expect to say something funny or spot-on at any moment. A dot of whip cream, from some cake he'd just eaten, stuck to his upper lip for the time being.

The sound engineer scratched his belly. It protruded from under his stained T-shirt, a hairy piece of human equipment that had evoked another fierce comment from producer Hitomi Sakamoto a half hour earlier.

"Can't you cover up that overproducing factory down there?" she had said. "It's polluting."

"Polluting what?" he had asked.

"Everything! You look disgusting. This is the worst T-shirt you have worn all week. Do you realize that guests can see you through the glass?"

"They can only see my upper torso, Sakamoto."

"Oh now it's a 'torso'?"

Fortunately for him, it had ended there because there was no time left. And once the show went live, Hitomi usually refrained from commenting on his looks and behavior in order to concentrate on the broadcast.

Nevertheless, he tried to draw his T-shirt further down, to cover up that belly or factory. But it was too short, so he ended up lifting his pants a bit and tucking his shirt in more firmly.

In the corner of his eyes he saw Hitomi Sakamoto enter the studio floor, with the guest of the evening right behind her. She brought the man, tall and eminent by his appearance alone, to the table where the bizz jockey was getting ready for the show.

Don pushed some buttons and from the studio speakers the sultry opening piano of "Passion" started to play exactly when Hitomi came in. He looked on closely to see if there was any response from his producer, but there wasn't.

Too bad, he thought. Maybe next time.

They were only moments away from the live broadcast.

===

The security officer entered the elevator after doing his rounds on the 84th floor. He walked in before the doors had entirely opened, so he didn't notice the three masked figures until he was actually inside the elevator. He backed off immediately, but the burglars lurked out of the little cubicle, jumping on top of him before he could reach for his gun or his stunner. In fact, the opposite happened: one of the unknown men in black grabbed his stunner and, well, stunned him. Electric bolts rushed through him and he went blank.

Four

From a pre-taped recording, the WCBN Radio announcer introduced that night's episode of the world's largest business talk radio show The Boardroom. An audience of some ten million people, worldwide, listened at different times during the day or night as the announcer's low voice went swiftly through the standard opening lines, pronouncing each word meticulously in spite of the speed.

"It's eleven o'clock. The city is dark, but the fire burns. It burns in the offices. It burns on Wall Street. It burns in the City. It burns on the Bund. It burns in Dubai. It burns in the factories and power plants. And it burns within us. Because we are the business and we all need redemption. This is the hour of delusion and today's truth. This is The Boardroom. Here is your prophet, the buddy and the bodyguard of every CEO, the Don Juan of every business babe. Here is the world's one and only bizz jockey. Here is your BJ: Carl Pappas!"

Leaning close to the microphone, Carl Pappas took over immediately. "Men and women of the business," he said, close to his microphone, "welcome to The Boardroom, where just like any other day we ask ourselves: where do we stand? If you know the answer, you may call now. But don't take this lightly; many went before you. Many were mistaken. And are grounded now, in court, in jail or in hell. A few moments from now I will introduce tonight's guest, who is already sweating on the other side of the microphone. And while we wait till our first caller comes in, let me tell you about this businessman who was on a trip in a communist country. He had a suitcase full of electric shavers in a part of the world where people didn't have that."

Across from Carl, on the other side of the table, his guest smiled.

But on the other side of the window, his producer Hitomi Sakamoto did no such thing. She cringed at the thought of another bad joke. It couldn't be helped; her influence on the bizz jockey was considerable, but he never consulted her on the jokes. Some of them came from Job Messner, she knew. Many of these jokes were bad; some unfriendly towards women, others were just rude or even macho or sexist, others were cliché, and so forth.

Hitomi stood straight as a pole, her arms crossed, her tablet with the show's details between her arms. She was not very tall or noisy, and she didn't have to be, because she got her authority from other sources. Her physique being one of those — every move she made betrayed how athletic she was, even if she merely turned her head or raised an eyebrow. Her black, shining hair, tied together in a ponytail, and her slim, black suit emphasized the power woman she really was. When close to her, most men at WCBN Radio kept a relatively low profile; much lower than with any other female colleague. Sometimes, someone like Don Wozniak would whisper "I can hear her six pack," but things rarely went any further. She was also a confusing character at times, when she switched from intimidating one-liners to Geisha-like movements of her hands.

"So he knocks on a door and someone opens and he says hello and opens up his suitcase, you know, being overly enthusiastic and all. So he says something about a wonderful mustache and how it could be shaved off quickly without irritating the skin. Then he sees it's actually a woman who opened the door, maybe because she has this standard, communist haircut, who knows. The husband pushes away his wife and steps forward and he punches the business man right on the nose, and he shouts 'This one's for you, grow your own red mustache!'"

Hitomi put one hand in front of her eyes.

===

In a room adjoining the central lobby, a security officer looked at one of the many black and white monitors.

He touched his headset. "Jack, the 87th floor is supposed to be empty, I see three people running through the hall."

"Did you say running? I'm going up."

"Where are you?"

"I'm in the garage right now."

Five

"I'm proud to introduce tonight's guest on The Boardroom to all of you business people. Ladies and gentlemen, the Secretary of Internal Affairs, responsible for all immigration affairs including border control, Anthony Plummer. Mr. Plummer, welcome to The Boardroom."

Plummer was a tall, official looking man. Not the boring kind though, for he brought certain movie star qualities to the job. His white hair waved around his forehead elegantly, his face was in the upper regions of attractiveness, the movements of his hands were controlled and subdued, and his suit was tailor made, of fine quality. The perfect representative of a government in modern times, constantly scrutinized and distrusted. Here was a man you would believe on face value.

However, this was radio, so none of these qualities had any chance of working in his advantage. And then there was also the bizz jockey, sharp and aggressive as always.

"Glad to be here," said Plummer.

"That remains to be seen," said Carl, lowering his voice further and picking up some grind. "Your field of expertise is facing strong winds these days and a lot of people are upset with what you are advocating."

"Well, what's your position then, Carl," said Plummer. "I am under attack on a daily basis, so let's get on with it."

"A lot of people feel that your quest for taking in more immigrants, granting more visas, is the easy way out," said Carl.

"Oh come on, bizz jockey," said Plummer. "There is no easy way out of this. People are talking about what immigration should be doing for us, which is not the point. We should be talking about what is going on over there. Why are these people fleeing, crossing the border, being abused by human traffickers, girls raped, babies being stolen, even organ theft? Why are they submitting themselves to that kind of violence? Because their situation at home is even worse. We are talking about countries where ordinary people have no safety. Where gangs rule."

"We know that, Mr. Plummer."

"These narcotics gangs are now turning their attention towards ordinary folks because they have been kicked out of drug trafficking by our government, and other governments. They are kicked out of business by brute force..."

"The war on drugs..."

"...and so they jump on ordinary people."

"So what's your point? We go along with it?"

"I am simply saying that WE ARE RESPONSIBLE, Mr. Pappas. The violence in those nations, the gang infested slums, the ultra violence that is inflicted upon families and children, all that is partially our fault. Well, it may not necessarily be our fault, but we are part of the spiral that caused it. WE use these drugs. WE buy them. And then WE put the narco gangs out of business. So the least we can do is reach out to innocent folks."

===

In the security office, Jack sounded through the speaker. "No one here. But I did find Ruben on the floor. He's unconscious, though he doesn't seem to be wounded. He's been paralyzed by his own gun. it's on the floor. I think you need to put out an alert. There ere people in the building."

Six

Two doors were kicked open with brute force, at the exact same time.

Carl Pappas had just announced a commercial break. Immediately after that, Don Wozniak had taken the studio microphone off the air. Then three men entered simultaneously; one went into the sound engineer's booth and the other two joined the bizz jockey and his guest in the studio. Black, shining automatic rifles were pointed at Carl Pappas and Don Wozniak at precisely the same moment. The third man, who carried his rifle on his back, said: "We are in control. Do exactly as I say and this will all be over within minutes. Do something stupid, and you have a bloodbath on live radio."

Both Pappas and Plummer had their hands on the table. Hitomi stood with her arms crossed. Don held both hands above his console, waiting, beginning to sweat under the cold touch of the gun's barrel against his temple.

"Proceed with the broadcast," said the man with the rifle on his back, pointing to Carl Pappas. "You, get out of the chair," he said to Flummer. Then he sat down in Plummer's place and positioned himself in front of the microphone. "Let's roll," he said and emphasized his point by drawing a circle in the air with his index finger. "Announce me."

Then the commercials ended and the live mike went back to Carl. The bizz jockey looked at the man in front of him. On the table were now a hand grenade and a Glock. Pappas moved his lips from left to right. His nose followed the movement. Then he proceeded. "All right folks, I interrupt our interesting conversation with Secretary Plummer for an important message. I am turning the mike over to an unexpected guest, who'll tell you all about it."

===

Philemon Solo spit out his last gulp of coffee across his desk on the eighteenth floor. He had a lot of documents to go through on his tablet and had decided to greet Secretary Plummer during the intermission half way through the show. But the security guard on the phone had jerked him out of his thoughts forcefully, right when a dark, barking voice started to interrupt The Boardroom on his radio.

Something was very wrong.

Solo instructed the security guard to go on full alert at once, involve the police and send all available staff to the broadcasting area on the seventeenth floor.

"But be careful, it sounds like a hostage situation."

A few seconds later he was talking to a friend from a secret law enforcement agency. "Bill, it's Phil. Warm up some choppers. I got terrorists in my building."

Seven

"We are the Immigration Block," said the man at the table. He read from a piece of paper and he did it fast. With one hand he held the paper, with the other hand he pointed the Glock at the bizz jockey.

There were only two people present who looked on with an uninterested lock on their faces: Carl Pappas, from the other end of the radio table, and Hitomi Sakamoto, from the other side of the window. Everybody else present had their eyes and mouths wide open, palm wet with sweat, hearts beating out of proportion.

My ratings are going to explode, Carl thought.

They are not here for the bizz jockey, Hitomi thought.

"...and we take a stand were our government sits back like a lazy fat pig. Instead of fighting the immigration tsunami that is wreaking havoc on our finances and our job market and our healthcare system, they propose weak laws to beckon more people across the border. It has to stop. This country should only allow the educated, the people who can contribute to our nation from day one. All these other vultures should be send back. We as Immigration Block say:

block immigration by stopping Mr. Anthony Plummer. His campaigning for free immigration is a crying shame. We are giving him our first official warning." After saying this, he got up.

In the engineer's booth, Don Wozniak was ordered to shut down all the microphones. They were off the air now.

"Hey, what are you doing, don't do that!" yelled Don.

One of the invaders was hovering over his console and pushed some buttons. On one of the control screens, yellow alert signs started to blink.

"Oh man, you've cut us off!" yelled Don.

But by that time the man with the rifle had left him and Hitomi, and was out the door.

"What'd he do?" hissed Hitomi.

"Nothing much. Just takes me at least twenty minutes of reprogramming before we can go back on the air, that's all."

Beyond the window, the studio was being evacuated rapidly. Carl Pappas sat alone behind the dead microphone as he watched Anthony Plummer being rushed out of the room under the threat of an automatic rifle and a Glock. They were gone within seconds after the termination of the broadcast.

Now that the door was standing open again, Carl finally heard the distant howl of sirens, deep down in the city.

===

Many floors up, Anthony Plummer got the scare of his life. His kidnappers had rushed him from the studio to a maintenance room and then into a shaft too small to hold a normal elevator, and had hoisted him up a cable at least a dozen floors upward. While the sound of sirens and screaming voices could be heard as echoes through the shaft, the Secretary and the three assassins moved up unseen, out of sight of cameras and running people.

Then they hauled him from the shaft, ran him through a corridor back into the room they had used to enter the building.

To Plummer's shock, the three of them buckled up hang-gliders. He wanted to say something, express his reservations, but he didn't get the time. He was buckled up too, tied to one of the assassins and then the other two helped them out the hole in the window; sort of shoved the two of them out.

On the floor, Job Messner was slowly coming back to life again.

Eight

"Enough!" shouted Carl Pappas.

Lieutenant Carlsberg of the city police department looked disappointed. Behind his back, his colleagues Homburg and Koster were talking to other WCBN Radio staff. The room, a meeting facility on the seventeenth floor, was buzzing and echoing with activity.

Carlsberg had dealt with the bizz jockey before and was generally under the impression they had developed a friendship. But that feeling was hardly ever confirmed. Still, he kept on trying the friendly approach time after time. Even this night, when federal police were stumbling around the crime scene, the government had already called his boss and threatened to have them all fired.

Fortunately, Carlsberg had had a solid upbringing. As the child of an army trooper he had been trained all his youth for one thing only: not to panic. He had stood in a burning barn, learning not to panic, waiting for his father to bail him out at the last second before his hair caught fire. His father's strategy to make a tough man out of him could have backfired easily and made a nervous wreck out of him, but it hadn't. He was subdued from the get go, under any circumstance. This weird night in the WCBN Radio building — when the whole world was acutely aware of the kidnapping of an important government official, and thus breathing down his neck — was no exception. He had thrown his Fedora on the table and stroke his mustache, a carefully grown thing that could mean he was quite a trendsetter for his age or utterly outdated. His brown raincoat gave him a cliché detective look, but times were changing. Facial hair had moved from hip to *verboten* in a century, and then from *verboten* to hip again in a couple of decades, so who was keeping the score?

"You can't put Job Messner on your list of suspects, that is ridiculous. He retreats to higher floors often because it is quiet up there. So he happens to be in the room where these kidnappers come in — big deal! Besides, he has nothing to gain from helping them."

"You can go," said Carlsberg, giving Messner a nod. The staff writer nodded back with his head, the white bandage already starting to show blood stains from his head wound.

"Who called in the federal police?" asked Carlsberg.

"That must have been Solo," said Pappas. "Listen, I can see this is leading nowhere. They came in and got out through the air, that's a neat trick. They left no traces."

"Except for one," said Carlsberg.

And, together: "His voice."

===

Ramon Rodriguez was tired. Finally he had some time to think, but it was difficult to organize his thoughts after the past weeks of chaotic travel. First the long walk to the border, hiding in the area in the hands of the organization that was going to escort them. Then the strange voyage across the border, then onwards and onwards through this vast land.

The neon lights were only partially filtered by the room's curtains, leaving just enough light to see everything that was there with sparse details. The blistered cupboard. The crooked chairs. The table, which was nothing more than a wallpaper table. The kitchen with the coffee machine and the one pit stove.

In spite of the run down state of affairs of the cheap motel, it all looked like a millionaire's mansion to Ramon. And what was more: he was convinced it looked like a billionaire's mansion to his wife and children. So far, they had been ecstatic about this temporary home on the way.

There had been questions, of course. Where are we going to live? How long will the journey take? Will we have a house? None of these questions could be answered with certainty, unfortunately.

Oh, he had plenty of family to go to, and probably would — but there was something on his mind that needed to be settled first. The violence, the abuse, the extortion, all the horrible things his family had had to endure in the past months, had settled on his gut like Chernobyl fallout on a field of spinach.

Someone needed to speak out and Ramon had thought about it and remembered this famous talk radio disc jockey, who had the world's largest audience and had a big mouth and was unafraid. He was the man they needed to talk to.

Yes, the bizz jockey was the man his wife and children were

going to tell their horrors to.

Nine

Boy, did he long to get out of the WCBN Radio building for a moment. Since the previous night press and public had gathered in the street and the lobby as if it were an anthill. Every half hour someone from the staff went down to speak through a megaphone and tell them all there was no news from the police department.

But it seemed pointless.

"They're not really interested in the kidnapping of a government official," said Phil Solo upon returning from yet another public speech in the downstairs lobby. "They're after your neck again."

Carl sat with his back to his desk on the seventeenth floor, looking down at the sulky day.

Yes, it's a *sulky* day, he thought. There are so many clouds that it doesn't even *look* like a day. So it's sulky. It's pissed off. And it is dragging us all down with it.

At the same time he waited for WCBN Radio's general manager to hit him below the belt. Because that's the way things were between them.

"Funny how even in the greatest crisis this station has ever endured, a hostage situation on live radio, in the end everybody wants to kick *your* ass. What is it with you that brings out the worst in people? There's a whole crowd out there that chants your name."

The bizz jockey jerked his chair around. "Oh come on Phil, quit beating around the bush. What are they saying exactly?"

Phil fell backwards into one of the chairs on the other side of Pappas' desk. "They are demanding that the bizz jockey starts a crusade against human trafficking."

"Typical," growled Carl. "There should be a crusade against government policies concerning immigration. Human trafficking is merely a result of that."

"Don't turn anti-government on me, Carl. Human trafficking is a disgrace."

"And it's all caused by the war on drugs. These cartels are moving away from drugs, towards ordinary people. In those countries, it's now becoming safer to extort families than it is to continue the drugs war."

"It's also less lucrative," said Phil. "I don't buy it."

"Who cares what you buy? This is what's going on. Is it that hard to see?"

"Changing the government's mind is virtually impossible."

"Did you say the government's *mind*?"

"Very funny, Carl. Just as long as you don't talk that way on the radio. It creates the wrong impression."

"I'm not worried about making an impression."

"I know. It has made WCBN Radio big. Just don't overdo it."

"Don't worry. I'll go after the human trafficking. I have no other choice."

"Try to leave out some of the gore. We are still a family

radio station."

They sat there for a while, looking out over the city. Points had been made, they were satisfied with it. They were good at sitting together and saying nothing, though it didn't happen too often. It felt good though. They were both professionals in the radio business, they knew they needed one another.

Not that they liked it one bit.

===

The container was comfortable, albeit cold. They sat on the cold floor with their backs against the metal, listening to the roaring of the truck's engine and the rushing of the wheels on the highway outside.

"That is a kind man, daddy," one of the children said.

But Ramon didn't answer. His thoughts were like a magnet, drawing him further across the land, to that big city where the bizz jockey resided. Indeed they had been lucky enough to find a truck driver who was willing to take them in the right direction. The sight of a poor family and its undernourished children had probably stirred a feeling deep inside the man. Perhaps some old guilt had reared its head and urged him to take the family in and offer them shelter in the container on the back of his truck.

Who knows, Ramon thought. And who cares?

He was rehearsing his speech for the bizz jockey. Or for the porter in the WCBN Radio building, because that would be his next border to cross. It all depended on finding the right words.

So he began again. This time, he decided to skip his

opening line "I beg of you." It just sounded too vulnerable. He was going to change that line into something powerful like "You are about to take the most important decision of your life, Sir." There. That sounded a lot better.

Ramon smiled in the semi-darkness, while the movements of the truck made his head shake.

===

The gray seemed to be seeping down from the sky and permeating everything it touched. Even though the day was well on the way towards adulthood, the trees stood almost colorless along the riverbank, as dull as the office buildings of the city's business district behind them. The grass, the flowers, the water, even the wooden exterior of the diner *Gulag* had lost all of its log cabin splendor.

On top of it all, a man who was normally unimpressed by weather, Mach One, sat abashed on the bench. He looked across the quiet surface of the river, an almost aluminum plain in front of him, awaiting the arrival of his client, the Bizz Jockey of WCBN Radio.

Thoughts of long gone adventures drifted in front of him, like ghosts dancing on the water. He saw old friends from his days in Siberia, men frozen to death. He saw someone riding a camel and an old buddy running through the bushes of Vietnam, only to be burned to a crisp by fire grenades falling from the sky.

Mach One was a little giant. Not too tall, but bulky instead. Now that his younger days were over, he no longer got the physical exercise he needed to match his diet, and he had grown fat. The old strength was still visible, but the old stress had stayed with him, like a ghost that wouldn't leave him. He sat nervously, as always, moving some part of his body without interruption. Today it was his right foot, making rhythmic movements, tapping the moist grass continuously. His hat held most of his dandruff together, though some of it had nested on his shoulders. His battered nose had a rouge shade and his upper lip scar protruded through his mustache.

He shook his head to dump the stream of images from his head. It had been an annoying experience, not to be repeated. He folded his collar upward and then heard the rushing of clothes when someone sat down beside him.

"Does this day suck," said the voice of Carl Pappas next to him.

Mach One turned his head. "It does. You know, for a change I agree with you. I don't know, suddenly I'm tormented by memories. So I'm counting on you to give me something useful to occupy my atrophied brain with."

"Don't worry, I got just the thing for you," said Carl. "What do you know about cartels that have shifted from narcotics to human trafficking?"

"Not too much," said Mach One. "I find that stuff too serious. In the old days, cartels were into basic crime. Now it's all become very inhuman. As far as I'm concerned they're all psychos."

"Are you getting soft now, Mach?" said Carl. "I've never heard you back off before."

"I'm not backing off," said Mach. "I'm just saying I don't like certain crime scenes. What are you after? You want me to find your kidnapped guest for ya?" He started laughing, a hollering sound that came from deep within.

"Glad to hear you're amused," said Carl. "You must be the only one."

"I'm already on it," said Mach. He lit a cigar and waved it in the direction of the river. "Nothing like a good job to keep your mind occupied and forget this grayness."

"I haven't decided what to do yet," said Carl. "The police are investigating the kidnapping already, I'm not sure if that's the direction I want to go. It's this whole immigration issue that is coming down on me, people want me to raise my voice. I just don't have a clue yet."

"Want to attack some cartels, is that it?"

The bizz jockey took Mach's hat and tried it on.

"Doesn't do you any good, bizz jockey."

"Guess not."

The hat changed heads again.

"Look around for me a bit, will you, Mach? I'll think about it, which way to go. Something will come to me soon. I have a lobby full of demonstrators I have to answer to."

Ten

They were standing under the sun, a hot golden circle above them beating down on the terrain as much as on them. Each of them was sweating like a maniac, except for the man with the nose.

Around them, the landscape tried to hide beneath the vibrating air that was sucking the last moisture out of the ground. The few bushes looked as dead as they could, as if they were about to turn to stone. There were crows nearby, screaming and flapping. In the distance, among the hills, was a small town, quiet in the afternoon. Mosquitos were buzzing.

The man took off his red dot and played with it by switching it from finger to finger, and rubbed his nose. He was a tall man, fat but muscular. A day's beard shaded his jaws. His hair was withdrawn, but the rest of it was thick and greased and combed back and his eyebrows were thick and dark. He wore an expensive suit.

He was leaning against an unremarkable car, a dusty terrain vehicle.

There were several other men and several other unremarkable cars. The men looked pretty much the same, dressed in black suits, hiding behind dark glasses. Slim, athletic and armed.

The argument was loud and aggressive — that is to say: men were talking loud and spitting, but not the man with the red clown's nose.

"The transport pendejos are responsible."

"We can't process so many people at such short notice. We don't have the capacity. Get it?"

"What happened to this organization? Have we sunk that far? You're supposed to fix it. Steal a trailer. Who cares? Just fix it."

"We move as much as a muscle and we have the feds on our back and you know it, moron!"

"Shut up!" shouted the man with the red nose all of a sudden. He had put the thing back on his nose again.

Which is precisely what they all did next. Except for one, who said "Mr. Angelos, I truly believe..." and then was shot in the forehead by the man with the red clown's nose.

"We can nót maintain our present power if we falter," he said, while putting the gun away again. "Don't forget that many other parties — and I mean not just the government — think that drug trafficking is for soldiers and human trafficking is for losers. The only way to stay on top of things is to be ruthless."

He took off his nose, bent over the dead man and put the red dot on the corpse.

"If you haven't the capacity for more people, get some. Come to me. What could be the problem? Money? Weapons? You need to hide more people? Come to me. Just don't sit there and do nothing and then complain about capacity."

From his coat he took another red clown's nose and put it on, adding a grin to it. "And for heaven's sake, don't take it so seriously."

There was some uncomfortable laughter, because Mr. Angelos' grin was truly a scary affair. As always, he reminded them all of a scary clown, all teeth and bloody dots, bending over them.

===

The restaurant was tiny compared to the immense parking lot that surrounded it. Endless rows of trucks rested, their engines ticking while they cooled down. Most trucks were abandoned, their drivers gone to the restaurant. But some were still inhabited. The cabin curtains might be drawn so that the driver could sleep. Several drivers might be sitting on impromptu furniture between their trucks and playing cards. Someone might be doing some repairs.

From the back of a truck that had just arrived, a family emerged. The head of the family shook hands with the driver in an elaborate ritual.

"You take it easy now, Mr. Rodriguez," said the truck driver, a bear of a man dressed in overalls. He made a wide gesture with his arm. "We're on the edge of a suburb. But if you walk that way, you get to the river and you can take the free ferry to the heart of it. You can be there within the hour."

Ramon Rodriguez and his wife and children turned and started to walk away.

"Be careful, you all. I wish you luck."

They turned and gave him a feint smile, but they didn't

stop walking.

Beyond them, in the distance, the gray shadows of the city's skyscrapers rose from the fields.

Eleven

In the corridor from the elevators to the bizz jockey's office, Hitomi walked towards Carl.

"Carl Evangelos Pappas, I must speak to you," she said.

Somehow, he thought, this woman knows my every move before I make it. She possesses an eerie talent.

He could tell Hitomi was preoccupied by something, for she looked around her, and down at the floor before she spoke.

"There are some people you must see," she said, looking up.

Pappas sighed. This type of introduction meant that she had invited people he really didn't want to see. Most of the time, the result was that he changed his mind about someone, but only after an embarrassing encounter. It was part of Hitomi's direct approach: seeing is believing. She felt that one can have no real opinion about anything until one talks to the people involved — and Pappas understood that, even though he didn't always like it.

"Who are they, Hitomi?"

"Immigrants," said Hitomi. She raised her hand and her

index finger to silence him before he had a chance to react. "Their story is unbelievable. It must be told."

"We'll see about that," said Carl as he turned and walked the remaining steps through the corridor.

With Hitomi on his tail, he opened the door and entered his office.

In the corner seating, a small group of people resided. A man, a woman and three children. The elders must have been in their early forties, the children young teenagers. They looked worn out, even the young ones were bent over or hung back. As soon as they were aware of their host and his producer entering the room, they sat up straight.

The man jumped up and rushed forward to shake Pappas' hand. "Mr. Bizz Jockey, it is my humble honor to meet you and I am very humble in the presence of your assistant Mrs. Hitomi for letting us into your office, being complete strangers and entirely new in your wonderful country. Please forgive the terrible intrusion on your work."

Carl wanted to say something in the line of courtesy, such as "that's quite alright", but he had trouble interrupting the man as he turned and made fierce gestures towards his companions. They responded by jumping up and moving forward.

Then the bizz jockey was surrounded by them.

"Please meet my family, who are equally humbled by your presence, Mr. Bizz Jockey. This is my wife Larissa... my daughter Carolina, my son Ruy and my youngest daughter Emmeline."

There was elaborate shaking of hands, there were even bows — but that was the limit for the bizz jockey.

"OK everybody relax," he said firmly. "Please sit down so we can all have a coffee or a soda or a tea or whatever you want. And ther. I would like you to talk to me about whatever it is that brought you here." He held the youngest child Emmeline's hand a little longer than the others'. "Because I think you have travelled a very, very long way for me."

The child nodded and the oldest child, Carolina, started to cry.

We were staying, Mr. Pappas, on a rusty cargo ship that was moored on a river bank. Probably because no one bothered to look at it. There were hundreds of containers on it and we were inside. We stayed inside during the days and were allowed on the deck at night. There was a little food and water and there were toilets, but we didn't know where we were and how long it was going to take. They put the ship on the middle of a lake so no one could get off. We stayed for two weeks on that ship. During that time, Mr. Pappas, Mrs. Hitomi, there were a hundred and fifty of us, I believe, and seven girls disappeared, three adult men were abducted and later brought back with a scar in their abdomen. We now know they were sedated and had an organ removed. Perhaps some of this occurred as payment, I do not know that. My family, we paid in advance so we were not bothered in that way. After two weeks we were taken off the ship in four groups during four consecutive nights. Two families stayed behind. We were in the last group and we heard screaming and shooting. I know they had problems paying the money to the people who were transporting us across the border.

Carl had to go to the men's room for a break and saw Hitomi

play with the children in the corridor. She looked at him with a feint smile.

She knows the entire story already, Pappas thought. Vicious little gym woman, lifting weights and getting me to sit down and listen to horror stories.

In the lavatory, he threw up.

But they did bring us safely across the border, and then we were on our own. We were lucky in that way, and the journey across your country was comfortable. But while we traveled towards family, I watched television in motel rooms and listened to the radio and I realized that the immigration issue that is beginning to suffocate our people is not understood here. People think our coming is a new gold rush, but it is not. Now that drug violence is subsiding as a result of the war on drugs, gangs are turning to abduction and extortion of ordinary folks. We have no defense. Something needs to be done, Mr. Pappas. I would rather return to my country than give up on it.

Later that day, Hitomi had a huge sushi dish brought up to one of the meeting rooms on the seventeenth floor and they all ate together and Don Wozniak and Phil Solo and Job Messner all joined and the mood was enlightened considerably. Solo and Messner had brought their pads and made sure the kids found some nice games to play. Sakamoto had Larissa join her in bringing the food around. Pappas and Wozniak were engaged in a lively conversation with the family's father.

"I like movies," said Ramon.

"So do I," said Don, releasing tiny sushi particles from his mouth, causing Hitomi to move further away from him, albeit slowly and unseen. "Which movie is your favorite, Ramon?"

"I like... I like Arnold Schwarzenegger," he said.

"Which one?" tried Don.

"I like!" yelled Ramon, apparently getting all worked up in a fit of enthusiasm that took his mind off his worries — something that was long overdue, no doubt. "I like Arnold! I like... *I'll be back.*"

"Yeah," said Carl, unsure about how to respond or how to get back to serious issues at hand.

But Don laughed. "Yeah, I like that one too."

They continued on the path of movie personae impersonations, but Carl's mind wandered off even more. He saw that the dusk had set in. The relaxed atmosphere could not hide the fact that time was slipping away. Not for the bizz jockey.

He also felt he was guarding the WCBN Radio building's windows almost continuously. Like the masked idiots of the Immigration Block were going to come in that way again, delivering the kidnapped Secretary of Internal Affairs, Anthony Plummer, back at his feet.

Or worse.

Twelve

If this gets any weirder, Carl Pappas thought, I'm going to demand a discount.

He was meeting with Mach One, who had for their meeting chosen an indoor swimming pool, a very old art deco building that was still run by the city. Which meant it was noisy and cold. It was clean, however, and at this time of day there weren't too many swimmers.

The giant hall towered over the pool, its glass roofs offering no protection from the grayness outside. They sat on the terrace, the only visitors, with an uninterrupted view of the pool.

"This is by far one of the dirtiest investigations I have embarked on," said Mach One. "Makes me uncomfortable."

"Good," said Carl. "That goes with the assignment and it proves my point. Found anything interesting I can work with?"

"That depends on your perspective."

"You know my perspective, Mach."

"I know it but I've never understood it. You go at it like a crusader, a modern knight, but at the same time it's business.

You have the shareholders of WCBN Radio to satisfy."

"Don't give me that," said Carl. "I have an obligation to fulfill, a duty towards my audience. That's how The Boardroom became big. They expect me to stand up and say meaningful things about immigration, and I want to, but I want to find the right angle. Adding mud to a dirt road is not going to pave the way."

They looked at each other; Pappas tried not to laugh while Mach One asked: "Adding mud to a dirt road... Is that an official saying?"

Carl looked at the pool, distracted, the stories from the Rodriguez family running a marathon in his head again.

Mach One sipped from his coffee. It was old-fashioned coffee without any of the 21st century additions with fancy names, as black as it gets. "This family was escorted across the border by the cartel of a man who goes by the name of Angelos. He's a big shot who built his own little empire in the drug business and seems to have disappeared from that scene altogether. He runs multiple transport routes and has been very evasive. But I have it from a deep source that his headquarters are established in... Well, a circus."

"Say what?"

"You heard that. I didn't believe it myself at first, but I've been able to locate the circus and it makes sense. It's a perfect hideout, I suppose."

"How do you know this information is accurate?"

"They also call him The Clown," said Mach, grinning at the bizz jockey's surprised face.

"Behind his back?"

"No. It's really a nickname. But no one would expect a

circus to actually be the headquarters of such a gang. I don't think there will be much going on there, but as a location it could be practical. Lots of places to hide stuff, you know, like paperwork and computer files and so forth."

"And if you know this, isn't this also known to the police?"

Mach coughed. It was so loud it was more like a bark. "Aren't you ashamed of yourself, bizz jockey? Can't you allow me a little bit of pride in my work? If this is known to the government, why would I charge you for it?"

Pappas wasn't touching his coffee. He sat with his arms folded, brooding.

"I've also analyzed the voice of the man who talked live on your show," Mach went on, "and it is clear that the Immigration Blockers, who kidnapped your guest, are operating as a separate branch of Angelos' cartel. He's not the kind of man you are going to locate just like that, though."

"I'm going to expose the suckers," said Carl.

"I'm not sure if you want to do that," said Mach. "You think you've seen what they're capable of, but you've seen no..."

"I've been told what they're capable of, Mach. Sure, the kidnap was the work of professionals. They're trying to influence public opinion and they're doing a good job. The higher the barriers at the border, the more money they can make trafficking people. But what they do with these people is far worse than this tinkering with public opinion. There is so much violence going on, it's devastating. If I can make one little wave in the ocean, I may have raised public awareness. It may actually result in something."

"Feel like swimming?"

"No I do not feel like swimming, Mach. What's your take on

the immigration issue anyway?"

"Don't do that to me, Pappas. I don't have a take on it. It's for politicians. You may have a point when you say that the war on drugs is partly the cause of it, but politicians are not likely to go blame themselves. Things will just stumble forward the way they always do."

"So it doesn't matter to you that you are making money on a case already lost?"

Mach One finished his coffee and got up. He took an envelope out of his jacket and put it on the table. "Are you in a bad mood or something, Carl? Don't take it out on me. I support you, you are a good man. Even if all your efforts sometimes lead you nowhere. But to take away any doubts you might have, I'm giving you this information for free this time. I do excuse your insulting remark though. I can see the stress you're under. Good luck, bizz jockey."

"What about Plummer?" said Carl with a sigh. He regretted his attack on the private detective.

"He'll be back," said Mach one.

A couple of minutes later, Carl could see the whale-like appearance of Mach One splash into the pool below, with a force that made other bathers look up, annoyed, and others swallow some foaming bathwater.

Pappas grabbed the envelope, took out the documents and started reading. It was never a good sign when Mach One felt bad about an investigation. It was not a good sign at all.

Thirteen

They weren't talking on the plane. Carl and Hitomi. It was basically just Don chatting away about his favorite radio shows of the past, like the famous live broadcast of *The War of the Worlds* that had caused a small but historical panic amongst the audience. He explained to no one in particular the limits of technology in those days, the mono broadcast, the type of microphone, the feedback problems and the expenses of keeping the taped recordings on file.

It was business as usual. Hitomi thought the whole operation was entirely ridiculous and irresponsible, that the bizz jockey had finally lost his mind, that Phil Solo should be told and so forth. The only reason she had come along was, in her own words, the safety of her boss, and she was doing it against her own will.

"You are not giving me any choice," she had said.

"Hitomi, don't play the innocent bystander, it doesn't look good on you. The only reason you are coming along is that you love a good radio story. You'll do anything for a good scandal on live radio," Carl had said.

"What I think I should do, is call Philemon Solo and have

him deal with this nonsense," Hitomi had said. "Looking up a cartel boss in his cave sounds like a suicidal act. Whether it sounds good on live radio or not. What do you think? 'I'm the bizz jockey so no one will ever harm me'? Is that what you think?"

So Hitomi had joined them like a young girl, sulky and reluctant and silent. It was indeed exceptional behavior for Hitomi, who was always in charge of herself, dealing with all affairs like a real pro. Except for the dangerous trips that Carl Pappas sometimes undertook; then the looming dangers sometimes shook her into an unpleasant temper that she only showed to Pappas and Wozniak.

But the men were used to this. They felt comfortable with the idea that their producer watched over them — and hey, they knew she would snap out of it real soon. She was not the kind of person to talk about what bothered her all the time anyway.

After a long silence, when the plane was descending after two hours, she said to Carl: "OK, here's the deal. Since I can't change your mind and since the only way I can look after you is going with you, I have thought about it and come up with a plan."

Carl smiled. "Does that mean you will now stop sulking?"

"Carl Evangelos Pappas, I do not sulk. I was whipping your butt."

"Of course you were."

"I am going to join the circus and assess the situation for you. From the inside, I can check things out."

There was a moment of silence in the midst of the rushing of the plane and the humming of Don Wozniak, who was now listening to one of the plane's radio channels through a headphone set.

"Pappas, your mouth is open."

"I was gasping for air. Sakamoto, it's in the middle of Friday night. We have till Monday afternoon before we have to be back. You think you can get a job in Angelos' circus at the snap of your fingers? That's not a workable scenario."

"Snapping my fingers is my specialty, Mr. Bizz Jockey," Hitomi said. She added the faintest smile.

And when Carl didn't answer, she said: "You may open your mouth again."

"We are on an important mission that goes way beyond our personal lives or the agenda of The Boardroom, or your agenda as a producer," said Carl. "By exposing that gang of dangerous criminals to the larger public, we may influence the outcome of the whole immigration debate."

"What outcome would you prefer?"

"Frankly, I don't really care. That's not the point. The point is to get things moving. Things are standing still. Ordinary people are trying to get away from a very violent situation in their hometown, they start on a journey to a part of the world where they can offer their children a better life, and then they fall in the hands of very dangerous people. By exposing that, we set things in motion. I don't think we can really determine the outcome, but setting things in motion is a good thing. Most of the time anyway. The immigration debate is in a cul-de-sac and things have to move back out of it. We can do something good here, Hitomi. Dangerous, but good."

He looked to Hitomi, who was looking at Don Wozniak in disgust.

"Danger is my specialty," said Don, while licking some pate from his thumb.

"Planes are too small for people like us," Hitomi sighed.

Fourteen

Crime likes rain, especially when it pours. The water blurs the view. Business that is better left unseen, can take place easier when clouds darken the sky and the water siphons the color out of the day. Then there are all the people who stay indoors on rainy days: the junkyard porter, the highway patrol man, the factory guard, the forester; those guys. Very convenient.

Another upside of a rainy day — from a criminal's point of view — is the noise, as Anthony Plummer could attest. He sat in the black limousine, its windows darkened, the rain hammering on the car's roof with such force that no amount of shouting or screaming in the world would draw any attention of people in the street.

No one could see him through the dark windows. No one would hear him through the rushing noise of the rain.

No one — if there was anyone, which there wasn't.

Poor Plummer. As a member of a family that had been in politics for a hundred years, he had been spoiled with security and safety all his life. The Plummer dynasty had brought on many members of government and congress, and Anthony had grown up in the presence of bodyguards and personal assistants. From his father he had learned a couple of bad habits, such as the occasional flirt with a personal assistant or a bodyguard, or the occasional one night stand or even an affair for a couple of weeks. But he had steered away from that behavior and kept a clean slate for a couple of years now. Anthony had understood just in time that in order to survive, in order to get anywhere, he had to keep up with modern times. Adapt to the new attitudes of cleanness, of correctness. His political career had been showing steady signs of upward mobility, and then this had happened. This... abduction.

Agreeing to appear on The Boardroom had been his undoing. That cursed Bizz Jockey! There had been no security in the part of the building where the broadcast took place. His own security people had been down in the lobby and the garage and the streets. But none of them had been close enough to protect him from these lunatics of the Immigration Block.

It was a funny name nonetheless. He could appreciate that. *Here's the Immigration Block and we're campaigning to block immigration.*

Everything else sucked. He had been treated like dirt.

"I am the Secretary of Internal Affairs," he had shouted when the masked men threw him into a tiny room after the long trip from the WCBN Radio building. He had been taken through the air under a man with a hang glider. Then across a highway while he was handcuffed inside a dark van. Then across some rough terrain and finally another hour in a helicopter.

That was the last time the men of the Immigration Block had allowed him something that resembled free speech. They had sealed his lips with duck tape and left him in the room with his hands still cuffed to his back.

Whenever he made a noise, like banging the door with his feet, two men came in. They were thick, muscular men with no visible traces of a neck, talking into cell phones almost all the time. To Plummer, there was no doubt that these men were not true activists.

They were mafia. Or they were cartel.

What's the difference anyway, he thought.

They moved around with that air of self-confidence, interested only in security. Paying attention only to controlling the situation and taking immediate action whenever the status quo was threatened. They had taken off their masks and never put them on again. Never did they engage in conversation, another sign that these people were not trying to convince anybody.

"We need you to be quiet, Mr. Plummer," one of the men said. "We will check on you with regular intervals, you know, so you can go to the toilet and stuff. There is no need to make noise. We've silenced your mouth. You don't want us to silence another part of you?"

That sounded like a line from a movie, Plummer had thought.

But the next time he hammered the door with his feet, they came in and gave him a severe beating. His nose bled, his face was covered with it, and he might have broken his knee.

"Please cooperate, Mr. Plummer," said the same man, who seemed to be the one assigned with the talking. "Or perhaps we should summon your wife to talk some sense into you? Or one of your children? Would that help?"

The limousine drove for an hour, then pulled up a gravel road and almost immediately halted. The two men got out of the car, walked to his door and pulled him out.

"You look a little pale, Mr. Secretary," said the speaker. "I guess it's time for you to get some fresh air." Then he grabbed Plummer's jaw with one hand and jerked off the duck tape with the other.

His pal removed the handcuffs.

"Please follow us."

Plummer looked around, his hands and mouth free for the first time in days, but he had been scared too much by these men to try anything.

If I run, they'll probably shoot me, he thought. That's the only excuse these thugs need.

So he followed his captors, while noticing the gray junkyard they were in. A desolate place, essentially a series of metal scrap hills towering around them. The only sound here was that of the rain.

What if they do shoot me here, Plummer thought.

When they reached a small shack without windows, one of the men opened the lock and led him in. The talker stood in the doorway of the dark cabin.

"There's a chair over there. There's a light. And there's a toilet. You'll be fine, Mr. Secretary. We will warn the authorities and tell them you're here within twenty-four hours. But there's a message for you from my boss. You have to slow down on the immigration issue. Opening up all borders is not an option if you want to stay healthy. We will come out of the night, like we did before, and make you understand if we have to. Don't force us to do that."

Plummer sighed.

"I think your children will agree with me on that," the man added.

"You leave my children out of this," shouted Plummer, throwing himself at the shack door, but it was already shut.

"Shout all you like," the man said.

Then it was silent.

Plummer was too tired to do any more shouting.

Fifteen

The *Orianapocatl* was clearing its throat. It was the largest volcano of the continent and had been dormant for almost a century. But now it rumbled under its snow-capped peak. Not that this worried anybody, because the rumbling was always very faint and it had been going on for about a decade now, filling the air with the sounds of distant thunder for a couple of hours a week.

In these past ten years more attention had been directed at its foot, where the border lay. Fences had shot out of the ground like fungus, rows and rows of them. Barbed wire, towers on the other side, trooper lights in the night and barking dogs. That and much more was a bigger concern to the local population than the volcano making some vague sounds every now and then.

The village of Orianoca, between the volcano and the border, had grown in that same decade and had stretched with a small suburb of improvised shackles and trailers. Most of the people who showed up here, left sooner or later, after they'd discovered that the border was effectively closed to ordinary people. Others stayed and went to work in one of the many factories in the area, where rubber was processed, and copper.

Close to the coast stood the hotel *Orianopl*, which triggered the bizz jockey and his sound engineer to speculate about the origins of all these Ori-names.

"Some conquistador wanted it to sound like Constantinople, no doubt," said Don Wozniak. "Isn't that obvious?"

"Don Lech Wozniak," Hitomi said, "that is the biggest nonsense I've heard since the last time you said something."

Carl couldn't help laughing, even if he was used to his sound engineer getting it from his producer.

"It doesn't even remotely sound like Constantinople."

"I think it refers to the Doppler effect," said Pappas. "In fact I'm sure of it."

"You mean Christian Doppler, the Austrian scientist who…"

"The two of you should be examined," said Hitomi.

Inside the hotel, white brick and red shutters in a sea of palm trees, they were unable to get any explanation from the manager behind the counter, so for the time being they gave up on trying to learn a history lesson. They all retreated to their rooms to get some rest after the flight.

Carl immediately activated his cell phone and dialed his boss, WCBN Radio manager Phil Solo.

"Plummer has been released, Carl," said Phil. "I can't tell you what a relief that is. The board members are finally off my back."

"I'll have Hitomi call him and set him up for a talk on The Boardroom," said Pappas.

"The hell you are," said Solo. "Do you think the Secretary has the slightest appetite to be involved with you ever again? The mere mention of your name will scare him away. He is so through with you. There's even a chance he will sue us."

"Sue us for what?"

"For failing to provide adequate security for a government official in our building, Carl."

"No one was expecting a raid through the windows on the seventieth floor, Phil. It's the kind of stuff that happens only in movies. It's too expensive to put people on every floor and those are your words. Well, I trust you've upped the security measures. But trust me, when I'm finished here, I got a bigger story than that. It will make Secretary Plummer think again."

"Big mouth, bizz jockey. Big mouth."

That ended their conversation.

Next thing he did was call home and talk to his girlfriend, but she was not there. He didn't feel like calling her cell phone and ending up not quite hearing what she was saying through the noise of a hipsters' cafe downtown, a photo shoot set or the dressing room of some dance club. He sent her a text message instead and then laid down on the bed to recover.

Which felt like Alice falling down the rabbit hole while holding on to dumbbells.

===

Finally, Hitomi had convinced the bizz jockey and his sound engineer that her plan was workable indeed. She had revealed a tiny part of her past life, the part where she had been a fanatic gymnast and done almost any kind of acrobatics one can think of. She was the perfect candidate for any circus job.

"Because that's the weak part of your plan," Carl had said. "You getting a job backstage. That usually takes a little more time than a Saturday morning."

"Not in the circus life," Hitomi had responded. "Trust me. There's always more work that needs to be done than they have people around. Listen, don't make a big deal out if it. All I need is to be inside the circus compound for twenty-four hours. I can manage that. You guys just go to the afternoon show to begin with. When you're there, I'll contact you during the intermission and instruct you. If there's something going on, we'll find out."

"Do circuses have intermissions?" Don had asked, looking puzzled.

"This one does."

The taxi that brought Hitomi to the circus entrance was shabby. This was a rich nation, but the border states were in decline. Too much money was flowing towards border security and prisons.

Illegal immigrants do not take cabs, Hitomi thought. Too bad.

Sixteen

Angelos was his real name, but he had lost his first name ages ago. People called him Mr. Angelos, or boss, or El Angelos, or Elang, but he had simply not been on a first name basis with anyone for at least three decades. It had become too dangerous to let anyone come close.

The secret services of at least five nations had been on his tail during his drug years. Those had been lucrative years, but violent as well. He had seen hundreds of his men die, and hear of thousands die. It had all come to a point where it was no longer a business he wanted to be in. It no longer required any brains, just a thirst for violence.

So he had steered his organization out of the business, making it look like they had lost power to other cartels and had withdrawn. The reality of moving into what he called *people's business* was kept hidden. It was a new territory, but it was a growing business and it required different skills. By now he had completely reinvented his act, dressing up like a clown and popping up in different circuses that his people had bought and expanded. With money from the cartel it had been easy to make the shows a little bigger, add some animals and cages and trailers and trucks for the purpose of hiding and trafficking people across the border.

His clown outfit worked well. No one in his right mind would go look for a godfather of a drug cartel dressed like a clown. *Working* as a clown, too. For a couple of years now this worked just fine. He had gotten the hang of making up his clown's face, the whiteness, the red sun. He liked the red dot on his nose and his costumes. He had assembled an entire wardrobe.

In between regular circus business he dealt with the 'other business'. That was easy. In several trailers were hidden spaces for communication equipment and his staff was part of the circus entourage as well.

Angelos' first man was the lion tamer. It was he who had put the idea into Angelos' head when he was thinking about changing business. He just mentioned it once, how he had worked as a lion tamer for a while when he was much younger.

It had been like the light of a nuclear explosion in the night, inside his head. The brightness of the idea still lingered with him.

Clown Angelos, fully dressed, walked to the main tent with the giant neon sign that read *Circus Oriano*. The outfit had been a local legend for a hundred years and they had gone out of their way to keep it that way. To change as little as possible. Only a few of the circus people were really involved in the Angelos' trafficking business. The rest was coerced into looking the other way. They had taken two members of the circus management out to the desert, have one bury the other in the dusty soil and spread the rumor delicately.

As for the local police force: the Angelos cartel had a long arm and if they suspected anything, he would know. Truth be told, the circus was on the outskirts of a large city and the police was simply not interested.

So that had been that. Everybody in the circus followed instructions to the letter. Some of the cartel's security men dressed up like animal keepers and kept an eye on things. All in all it was a successful operation, albeit one that could be exposed easily. So they were more on guard than ever before — but other than that, life was a lot less violent. In the three years since they had taken over the three circuses, no cartel member had died.

"What's on the agenda, Ages?" he said to the circus manager and ringmaster, as he entered the main tent, all dressed up in his clown's costume.

"Auditions," said the ringmaster. "We're short on staff and we need to hire at least a cook, someone to clean the animal cages, a waitress and an assistant to the trapeze team." He was an old timer in his last years, and he looked tired, but he had a huge amount of experience and he kept the circus going for Angelos. He did that with skill and efficiency, not with enthusiasm.

"You can learn from that man," Angelos sometimes said to his men. "He does the job, he doesn't fake joy. Joy is irrelevant."

They sat on the first bench of the ring. Mr. Ages yelled something and the first applicant walked in, a slim oriental woman in her forties. Angelos raised his eyebrows as she strode towards them with obvious confidence.

"I understand you need someone to step in with the trapeze team this very evening and blend in," she said, before any of them could speak.

Angelos gave Mr. Ages a little bump with his elbow.

"Now, Miss Sakamoto," said Mr. Ages. He looked at the clown next to him, and then back to the woman. "You have all the qualifications we need. I suppose it is not really necessary, but I just need to see you climb the pole to the platform and stand there a bit, maybe do some hanging over the edge. You're not supposed to do any real trapeze work, just assist the team, but I must witness you up there before I decide."

"It will be my pleasure," said the woman. "Should I be funny as well?" she said to the clown.

But she did not wait for his answer as she turned and attacked the pole.

Angelos realized his mouth was open and closed it quickly before Mr. Ages would notice.

Seventeen

The clown escorted Hitomi to the dressing trailer. He held her elbow lightly when he asked: "Do you have a lot of circus experience, Miss Hitomi?"

"Light years of it," said Hitomi, "Mr. ...?"

"Call me Angelos," said the clown.

He smiled, although that's always hard to tell on a clown's face. A clown can look sad or happy, but his makeup will always dominate with its huge red smiling mouth.

"Where's the rest of your name?" said Hitomi? "I think a real man has at least three names. Don't disappoint me now, clown."

"What the heck," said the clown. "Call me Angel Angelo Angelos, for all I care. But you're the only one."

They reached a large trailer. Angelos reached up to the door and swung it op, gesturing Hitomi onto the stairway.

"You're the first clown I've met who is involved in a circus management," said Hitomi, while she stepped up. "There's a serious side to you then, Angel Angelo Angelos?"

"Yes there is. I'm not even remotely funny in real life," said Angelos. He followed Hitomi up the stairs, his eyes fixed on her slim silhouette as it moved into the darkness beyond. "There's only one man on this planet who is more serious than I am."

They stood in the half-light of the trailer's interior. Rows and rows of clothes racks filled with outfits, from clowns and trapeze artists to the plain overalls of the service staff. An old man appeared from the back to take orders from the clown and then disappeared again to get the requested outfit.

"Who is that man, then?" asked Hitomi while they waited.

"My father," said Angelos. "May his soul rest in peace. He was always a serious man, but now that he's dead, well... I don't believe the afterlife is a very funny phase. You know, with all the penitence going on."

"Your father was that bad in life?"

"Yes," said Angelos. "I can't think of a single good deed he ever did."

The old man beckoned them.

In the back of the trailer was a changing cubicle.

"This is my smallest size," said the old man. He looked at Angelos with disgust.

While Hitomi took the clothes and stepped into the cubicle, Angelos said to the old man: "If it doesn't fit..."

"It'll fit, clown. It'll fit."

Hitomi didn't bother to close the curtain while she undressed.

The old man walked away, leaving Angelos staring at Hitomi's appearing slimness — and her unsmiling, straight face. She looked the clown right in the eye.

Angelos regained himself and turned away. "I'll wait for you outside, Miss Hitomi. When you are ready, I will take you to your quarters."

Eighteen

"The show must go on," said Don Wozniak to Carl Pappas.

The two of them sat on the third row of the circus, moving their knees to the side every time someone wanted to pass them on the way to an open seat. The arena smelled of saw dust and horses. The music was a whole different ball game.

"That's no excuse for pouring this horrible muzak over innocent people," said Carl. "Let's just pray the real show starts real soon, before they do more harm to my ears."

The tent entrance was being closed.

"Pay attention," said Pappas. "I see a whole series of empty seats. You notice it. There are ten chairs over there. And there. And..."

"Forty empty seats," said Don.

Carl stopped counting. "OK, forty. Listen, I am a little worried about Hitomi. No news from her since this morning."

"She said if there's no word from her, things are going according to plans," said Don. "You know Hitomi, she's in charge."

"From your point of view maybe," muttered the bizz jockey. "I'll want to see her before I believe that. I'm beginning to regret agreeing to her plan. If this place is indeed the lion's den, then she's in a really dangerous situation."

"Agreed," said Don. "These are the kind of people that do the stuff that Hollywood won't put to the big screen because they are too chicken."

Carl looked at his sound engineer with a big question mark on his face.

"You know, like ripping out..."

Wozniak was interrupted by a thundering musical theme from the sound system, a tune that attacked every single ear in its proximity with a predator's ferocity. The lights went down simultaneously and an old man in a white suit with a tailed jacket and a hat that was half a meter high, stepped in the heart of a spotlight. He commenced announcing the world's greatest circus, which was of course a joke, but he put his heart in it anyway and that gained him the sympathy of the bizz jockey and his sound engineer. For a moment they forgot their worries and looked on as horses ran into the arena, girls in trapeze outfits on their backs, twelve of them in a long row, whirling round and round.

They were shaken out of their temporary dream when they saw Hitomi Sakamoto climb up on the pole towards the tent roof. She was dressed like a professional trapeze artist, but she stayed on the platform halfway up, assisting a team that performed a series of breathtaking stunts in the air. They flew around like white birds, lifted up by strong arms and floating through space, to be received by another pair of strong arms across a void.

Carl looked at the circus people on the arena floor, the acrobats and the clowns and wondered which one of these people was the man they were looking for. There was no way of telling. They were going to have to wait for a chance to catch up with Sakamoto.

"Of course it's all nonsense," Don interrupted his thoughts. "How can you smuggle people in and out of a circus? You can't do it without being noticed. And these clowns all look dumb."

During the break in the middle of the show they got themselves some coffee, but they didn't catch up with Hitomi. Carl was working himself up over this. He touched the inside of his jacket to see if his cell phone was still there — the urge to call for outside help was getting stronger.

But it was the ever-present coolness of his sound engineer that moved everything forward again.

"Remember there were forty empty seats during the first half of the show?" said Don. "Take a look at them now." While he spoke he ate the remains of the donut he had bought with the coffee.

Indeed there were no longer any empty seats. It was now a full house.

"Can you identify someone who wasn't here before the break?" said Pappas.

"No way man. It's just more audience."

"It's possible they sneak in forty people each night. They mingle with the main audience and after that they leave the circus within a crowd. No one will notice."

"Sure," said Don. "That'll work. But the question is: how do they get across the border, into the circus? Besides... well, I don't know. No one said they smuggle people here. It's supposed to be the cartel's headquarters, that's all."

Nineteen

The audience had left. The neon lights above the circus entrance had been turned off. The food trailer had also been closed and the smells of sausages and hamburgers and hotdogs and coffee had faded with the heat of the day. The cold and damp of the early night were beginning to take over.

Hitomi sat in one of the many trailers that were parked behind the circus. Mr. Angelos had invited her to join him for a drink after the show. As soon as they had arrived in a trailer, along with the other clowns, she was left in a living room that resembled a small cantina. It was old and rugged; some worn out chairs were placed around a worn out table. There was a lamp and there were closets for clothing, not much else. Hitomi sat at the table and waited, while the group of clowns retreated behind a door and put up a group discussion that she could hear through the wall.

It was obvious to Hitomi that whatever it was they talked about, it was not ordinary clown's business. From intonation and mood she could detect a lot. She had known real clowns; they were either serious people who hid most of that behind uninterrupted banter — or they were silent and drank. Her favorite clowns were Russian; they looked sad and old, but could tell you the finest stories and knew the best liquor. Hitomi was not the drinking type, but she could appreciate a man who knew his drinks.

After fifteen minutes they all came back and rushed out of the trailer. Only Angelos joined her. He took out a cigar and started to light it.

"I must apologize," he said. "It is not my habit to keep a lady waiting. I hope you don't think I am uncivilized."

"The world is full of clowns," said Hitomi, putting a smile on her face that was very unusual for her. "Don't be too hard on yourself."

Angelos took two glasses and a bottle out of a cupboard and poured them both a bourbon, which he then offered to her while he sat down.

"Don't mind the makeup," he said. "I'll take it off in a moment. When we have finished our drinks. We have deserved it, you know. This show is hard work and for you, well, it was your first evening. I must congratulate you."

"Thank you," said Hitomi. "But it was nothing."

They lifted and touched glasses.

"Sometimes it is hard," said Angelos, while he took out a handkerchief and started to wipe the makeup from his face. His overkill smile melted like watercolor, giving him an even sadder look.

Hitomi was taken over by his new appearance; she felt a shiver. The unmasking of a man is not something to be taken lightly, but it takes a sensitive woman to take it in, to really notice it.

"Why?" said Hitomi. She walked around the table, sat down

on a different chair, took the handkerchief from Angelos' hands and took over the removal of the makeup.

A nerve twitched underneath his right eye. "I don't know," he said. "The circus life... is at the same time more relaxing than any other life I've known, and at the same time there is the sensation that an elephant might step on my foot, or a grown man might fall from above and crush me. The tent could collapse and a four hundred kilo pole might fall on my head. The audience might panic and trample me on their way out. I've never had fears like this when I was armed and dangerous."

Hitomi's hand paused for an instant.

"Yes, I was once armed and dangerous."

"And now you're not?" said Hitomi, proceeding with wiping Angelos' face.

"Not when I'm in the tent, no," said Angelos. "The rest of my life hasn't changed, but when I'm all dressed up and I enter the tent and the lights are on me and the trapeze artists are above me and I smell the elephants and the tigers, then a change comes over me."

"You are afraid when you are in the show."

"I'm a new man, that's what I know. People are laughing when I come in. No one has ever laughed before. When I came in, people wet their pants. Or they would greet me with a straight face. Now kids yell and cheer. I don't know myself when I'm in there." He had been looking Hitomi in the eye while he talked, which had felt kind of natural — but now that he had finished, it took over the moment completely. Everything else faded from the circus trailer.

Angelos had never been a womanizer; that is to say, he

never really acted on it. He knew women found him fascinating for a variety of reasons. He was the older, handsome man still in his prime. He was mysterious. He was powerful. All men treated him with respect or fear. That is the stuff that is attractive to some women, but he was interested in one-night stands nor serious relationships. His energy had always poured into the business; the cleverness of it, and the violence. There were women working for him, and sometimes he took in their beauty and their power and their friendship, for what it was worth. He saw himself as a man who would one day settle down and perhaps start a family, live in peace.

And then out of the blue there was this slim, short, powerful woman who gave him this faint smile — fainter than any female smile he had ever received — and he found himself confessing about his inner insecurities.

So he corrected himself, took his eyes off her and stood up. "I have an errand to run," he said. Then he added a smile to that, because the whole situation confused him and he wanted to soften some of his sudden rudeness. "I'm sure you want to relax a while after this show. Why don't you go to your trailer and I will look you up in about an hour?"

Hitomi nodded.

It was just the kind of break she was looking for.

Twenty

The night wears a different robe in these parts, Hitomi thought. The blackness is deeper, yet the stars are brighter, rich with contrast, as if there was more life here than in the city, where the night resided numbly over concrete and glass, and the odors of kerosene and gasoline, of alcohol and bratwurst.

The half-moon provided her with the right amount of light; she could follow the silhouette of Angelos across the circus terrain and still remain invisible in the shadows herself. The man walked through the forest of trailers and trucks until he reached the farthest area. There stood the trucks with the cages for the lions and the elephants, the cheetah and the snakes, and the dogs, and of course the horses. It was a noisy area, for there was always some animal screaming or roaring, or hammering a paw or a hoof.

On the other side of the cages, all of them on top of trucks, stood Angelos and his fellow clowns. Automatic rifles shone in the light of the moon and the stars. They were not talking. They smoked cigars and cigarettes and were looking up.

There was nothing there.

Or... was there?

After a while Hitomi thought her eyes had been compromised during the circus show. She saw groups of stars disappear and then appear again. It was happening in at least three places in the night sky.

It took her a while to realize something was approaching. Something that made no sound and was kept entirely in the dark. If it hadn't been for the clowns looking up, she might never have noticed.

Twenty-one

Only when the objects came plunging out of the sky all of a sudden did Hitomi notice what they were. She saw the group of clowns — some ten men all together — run around to assist the landing movements of three giant helium balloons.

Their baskets were filled to the brim with people, but everyone was very quiet. That was the signature of the operation: it was all done in almost complete silence, the only audible thing being the rushing of large propellers that steered the balloons; and the bump each basket made as it hit the ground.

Neither balloon stayed on the ground very long. The people were rushed out of the baskets by the clowns, their automatic rifles held high in the air to make any instruction redundant, and then all of them — a couple of dozen — ran away into the darkness, towards the cages and the trucks and the trailers.

Under cover of the night, they split up in several groups and disappeared in different directions. Hitomi stayed put and watched the balloons as the pilots steered the propellers, moving the balloon upwards again. Within moments the balloons were off again. This made a little noise, but the roaring of the lions, and the trumpeting of one elephant, behind them, was much louder. And up they went.

Hitomi withdrew from her hiding place under a truck, gave the scene a last look, only to notice that the balloons had become black holes in the night sky again. They would be a mile away within minutes.

As she crawled from underneath the truck and got back up on her feet to follow the troupe, she wondered about the operation she had just witnessed. Obviously the wind blew from across the border most of the time. The presence of the ocean in that direction made that almost a certainty. They could fly the balloons across pretty much whenever they pleased and then land the balloons somewhere else and ship them back across the border in a truck or by some other means of transport.

It took Hitomi a while to find the refugees again. Most of them had disappeared on the circus terrain, but a small group escorted by one of the clowns was standing next to a cage-truck. All the clowns wore a distinct outfit, with a dominant color like bright yellow or pink or red, but there were no colors in this night. So it could be any clown; anyone but Angelos, as he was taller than all of them.

It was a giant truck, which held several cages. Inside were the predators. Hitomi couldn't see everything in the dark; the refugees mounted a small stairway and disappeared through a door into the truck's interior.

A lion roared and there was the sound of a whip.

A woman screamed.

There were some hammering noises, another roar and then it was silent.

Finally, an armed clown and an animal trainer emerged. The trainer locked the door and the two men hurried away in the dark.

Hitomi sat in the dark for a moment, contemplating the scene. The cage-truck stood silent in the night. The only thing she knew for certain, was that some people from one of the balloons, perhaps a dozen of them, had gone inside the truck filled with lions, and were residing there for the time being.

No one could see Hitomi Sakamoto smile in the darkness; but the smile didn't last.

In the distance, the *Orianapocatl* rumbled.

Hitomi remembered how the hotel manager had said the volcano was merely 'clearing its throat'.

"Clearing his throat my butt," she whispered as she withdrew from the scene once again.

It was time to return to her trailer, text the bizz jockey about her discoveries and await the arrival of Mr. Angelos.

Angel Angelo Angelos, she thought, trying to taste the name as she pronounced it in her head. You crazy clown.

She smiled again, but the *Orianapocatl* roared and interrupted her thoughts. This time, she could smell the thing.

===

In the silent middle of the night, the banging from the lions' cages was unmistakable. Fists on wood. After a while, two lions started to complain, barking and roaring and getting up to do some walking back and forth, and it didn't take long for three men dressed in overalls and carrying rifles across their shoulders to appear. Two climbed the steps and entered the truck.

From the inside the sound of a whip could be heard. It snapped through the night, as if a rhythm section joined in to create some serious harmony in all the noises of the night: the roaring of the lions, the rumbling of the volcano and, additionally, the screaming of a girl.

From the pitch-black shadows of the trucks and the trailers a man approached. It was unclear if he was curious about the screaming girl or if he was just taking it easy, strolling through the night for a smoke. Whichever it was, the armed man by the lions' truck told him to take a hike.

"And make it snappy," he added.

The night stroller disappeared in the shades much faster than he had appeared.

The screaming stopped and the two men appeared from the trailer again. Within moments, the scene was empty again, and as if orchestrated, all other noises were gone too: the volcano held its breath and the lions and the girl and the rest of the people in the truck made no sound.

It was silent again, but it was a silence before a storm. Nobody in their right mind, had they been present, would dare to doubt that. Not even for a minute.

Twenty-two

"I don't trust that volcano," said Pappas at breakfast, as the hotel owner poured him coffee. He pointed towards the *Orianapocatl* with his knife. Butter fell off, but the bizz jockey didn't notice.

"It has been making these noises for a year, Mr. Pappas," said the hotel owner. "It means nothing. It is harmless. Trust me, it has cleared its throat last night and now it can sleep for weeks."

While he walked away, Carl muttered to Don: "They all talk about the volcano clearing its throat as if it's some local bar visitor who smokes too much. If that thing blows this place will disappear from the face of the earth within half an hour."

"You worry too much, Carl," said Don, in between taking bites from something that looked like a croissant but had the viscosity of cheese. "Listen, I checked it online last night when it woke me up. The scientific data gives no cause for alarm. It's just something deep within that's supposed to fade over time. Happens all the time, has been for the last two thousand years." He stretched his arm and lifted the spilled butter from the table with his thumb. "Any news from Hitomi though?"

"I thought you were never going to ask," said Carl with a grin. "She's on a major breakthrough. Listen, we are going to the show again this afternoon to put stuff on tape. Bring your recording equipment, the smallest stuff you can carry around without anyone noticing it. When we get these clowns on tape, we are going to go live with a killer revelation. It is going to set the news on fire. It is going to send an elephant into CNN's newsroom. People are going to scream bloody abuse."

"And you'll be even more famous than you already are," chuckled Don. "Don't ya love it? Boy it will be good."

===

Hitomi was going through a steamy affair. She was standing in the bathing trailer for circus personnel, the interior dripping with moisture from the ceiling and the walls. She had woken early to avoid the busy morning traffic when all staff members were late for duty, but even at this hour the showers were all running. The part she enjoyed was the part where no one gave a damn about a newcomer. From every job she had ever had, Hitomi remembered how she had been scrutinized on the first day, asked a million questions, walked the high wire towards acceptance. Here she blended in and there wasn't a single comment.

Which didn't mean she didn't attract attention when, as she stepped out of the shower cubicle with only a towel wrapped around her muscular body, moving through the steam in her athletic stride. All women were athletic here, so that was nothing special. No, it happened when a clown barged into the shower area and walked towards her.

There were protests from all other women.

"No men allowed, dammit!"

"Get out, you clown!"

"Being a school boy learning how to be a clown doesn't give you a ticket into the ladies department, you joker!"

But he had eyes for Hitomi only.

"Mr. Angelos is expecting you, lady," the clown whispered in her ears, as he grabbed her elbow.

That was a mistake. Two seconds later he was on the floor, bleeding from his purple horror of a nose, on all fours.

Hitomi, holding his arm on his back, whispered in his ear: "Don't. Touch. Me."

Applause thundered through the women's bathroom as the clown got up hastily and left.

Hitomi picked up her towel again. She didn't like drawing that much attention. Perhaps the reflex had been a little over the top.

Twenty-three

The afternoon show went smoothly. Basically the circus ran the same routine as the previous night, with slight alterations, some of them intended for the increased amount of children among the audience.

But it was an enjoyable performance again, so Pappas and Wozniak left the tent with a certain amount of reluctance. Playtime was over; they were shifting into gear. First mission: to get out of the crowd and onto the circus terrain unseen — and as fast as possible.

In the area where drinks were served, they walked towards the public toilets. Hitomi had given them precise instructions, and they all added up.

Both men went to a separate toilet.

Carl locked the door and took a package he had been carrying under his coat. It was an overall with the circus logo on it. Within moments, he changed into the yellow outfit and left the cubicle.

In the back of the toilet trailer he joined Don Wozniak. There was another door back there. It was hidden behind a curtain, but it was there, and it was unlocked. The both of them dressed in overalls, they simply moved through the curtain and the door, and nobody paid any attention.

Behind the toilet trailer, Hitomi stood waiting. As soon as Pappas and Wozniak had arrived she walked them away from the public area.

"The trafficking takes place where the animal cages are," she said. "I cannot dig deeper, I have to prepare for the second half of the show. Also I must urge you to be careful. They may look funny, but these people are no clowns." She pointed them a direction by lifting her chin. "It's a hundred meters in that direction. See you guys later."

And she was gone behind one of the trailers. It was a crowd of wheeled houses stretching in all directions.

"Look busy," said Carl as they started to walk in the designated direction. He looked at his sound engineer. "You're not looking busy, Don."

"I'm not very good at that, I'm sorry. How should I... you know... do that?"

"Widen your eyes. Don't look around you like some tourist but focus on the horizon. Like you're going to war or something."

Wozniak followed the instructions carefully.

"Think of bloody clowns. That'll help. You know, the red on the lips is blood instead of makeup."

Don shook his head. "That's gross. I'm already feeling very busy, like I'm running away from something." In the back of his mind images started to pop up, scenes from his childhood when his teacher became furious at him, annoyed by his ever-relaxed attitude. There's nothing that enrages an enraged man more than a guy as relaxed as Don Wozniak.

But there was no time to think this over any further. The bizz jockey gestured him to remain silent and press against the side of a trailer.

"What?" whispered Don.

"They're taking out the lions. That's good. Gives us the opportunity we need."

They looked around a corner. Two animal trainers were escorting a lion and two lionesses out of a trailer and walking them in the general direction of the main tent.

As soon as the animals and their guards were gone, Pappas beckoned his sound engineer.

Don took out a tiny microphone and pinned it on his boss's jacket. Then he nodded.

"This is Carl Pappas, your bizz jockey," Carl spoke into the microphone as softly as he could. "We are standing on the grounds of the Circus Oriano, stationed in Orianoca. In the background you can hear the sounds of lions. They are being walked off towards the main circus tent right now. This means their cage is now empty. Don Wozniak and I are now going into the lion's den to investigate because if our suspicion is correct, the animal cages of the Circus Oriano serve a peculiar purpose."

Then Pappas drew a few quick circles in the air with his index finger, indicating to his sound engineer to continue recording.

"We're moving towards the cages now."

For two men on unknown and possibly dangerous territory, they walked with surprising grace. And that proved to be a wise choice, because they passed one man on his way to somewhere, who saw nothing but two men in overalls crossing the terrain. Nothing worrisome there, although that time would come. The volcanic rumbling in the distance emphasized that — but the bizz jockey and his sound engineer were too focused on entering the lion truck to notice.

As we all know: all negligence comes to an end.

Twenty-four

The enormous truck stood silent on the edge of the circus terrain. Beyond it, an open, dusty field stretched towards the fence surrounding the area. On the field stood several pieces of animal training equipment, but other than that it was deserted. In the distance, the volcano *Orianapocatl* rumbled and let out a tiny plume of smoke that rose in the air like a pillar. It was almost white and looked more innocent than it probably was.

On the back of the truck stood a container with air vents on the sides and a large tailgate at the end. The container was not just long, it was unusually wide as well. It was too wide for normal transport. The grass growing around the wheels indicated that migration was very unusual for this vehicle anyway.

The tailgate stood open and the bizz jockey and his sound engineer walked right in to inspect the cages.

There were four of them, each empty but the last one. A lioness lay quietly in the vague lights, looking at the visitors uninterested. Carl watched as Don walked into one of the empty cages.

"Our sound engineer is now inside one of the lion cages," whispered Pappas in his microphone. "It's completely empty, but it remains unclear if there is any hiding space for immigrants. We'll check the walls of this cage..."

He moved into the cage as well.

Don knocked on one of the walls. "We should measure the outside of the truck and see if there's a space between the walls."

Carl stamped on the floor. "Or underneath the floors."

They looked at each other dumbfounded.

"I definitely hear something below," said Carl into his microphone. "Now that means either some animal under the truck or..." He turned to Don. "Come one, we have to hide. If there's people down there, it won't be long before we can see them."

They hurried out of the cage, the sound engineer wondering what the rush was about all of a sudden. But he had learned to trust the bizz jockey. So he followed suit.

===

From behind the curtains in the main tent, Hitomi saw the lions arrive in the outside cage. At the same time, a group of clowns left the circus and hurried, armed and all, in the direction of the animal cages on the edge of the terrain. Things were going as planned. Any moment now, the radio detective would unearth the precise details of Angelos' operation.

Twenty-five

From under a canvas, draped over a series of crates, Carl Pappas and Don Wozniak looked on as the clowns entered the lions' truck. They were laying down on the wooden floor in an uncomfortable way, but the sights and sounds made it well worth the while The armed men, six in all, walked right into a cage in the middle of the truck and jerked open a floorboard. What ensued was a noisy affair, which made Pappas imagine enormous ratings and a momentary satisfaction on the side of WCBN Radio's shareholders. Although it must be said he didn't like thoughts of the shareholders intruding on him.

This proof is going to solidify my show for another decade, he thought, but immediately he was embarrassed as he witnessed the condescending way in which the clowns treated the people who now emerged from the hidden space below the animal cage's floor.

There was shouting, there was jerking, there was threatening.

"Move faster, you moron," — that sort of language.

And now it was all recorded.

After a while, thirty people had climbed up, to be escorted

out of the truck. It all happened very fast.

When the truck was empty again, Pappas and Wozniak crawled from under the canvas.

"What you just heard," said Carl into the microphone, "were the immigrants crawling out of a secret space underneath the cage floor. They were then escorted by a group of clowns from the circus and, as we suspect, taken to the main tent to join the audience. It is now three thirty PM."

He nodded to Don, a sign that the recording could be stopped.

They hurried out of the truck, only to assume their circus personnel posture again, and walk back to the toilet truck before the show started its second part.

"They're all sitting over there," said Carl in his microphone. "I recognize some of them at least."

Pappas and Wozniak were sitting in the audience on a high ring of seats. The bizz jockey was reporting again, spilling important details on the recording that Don was making. No one in the audience around them noticed. There was too much noise. There was the circus music coming from the speakers, there was the cheering and laughing. Nonetheless, the delicate recording equipment would pick up the bizz jockey's every word.

A little to the left, where the empty seats had been during the first half of the show, the refugees from the animal cage sat. They were a funny lot. Of course, the last thing they were interested in, was a circus performance. Obviously to Carl, these people loathed the lions' act. But they must have been instructed to act like regular audience, and so they joined in the laughter and the cheering as well as they could, all of them: old men and woman, younger parents, and several teenagers and children.

The bizz jockey felt sorry for them, but he felt no rage. There was too much noise, too much excitement going on. Although he felt comfortable with the prospect of broadcasting this whole charade, he also felt doubts. If these people endured so much to cross the border, was he doing the right thing trying to dismantle this organization? It served a political purpose; it remained to be seen if it truly served these people in the near future.

Twenty-six

They were standing behind the main tent. Once again they had changed into their circus overalls, but this time they felt less comfortable. The audience was leaving the terrain, which meant that their cover was gone. Between now and the evening show, they were alone amongst the circus personnel.

"I need to find a place to upload the recording," said Don.

"It isn't uploaded yet?" gasped Carl. "Why not?"

"There's no network here," said Don. "I mean, I did have network connection for moments on and off, but it's just too weak. I need to get to a terminal connected to a landline. That's the only way."

"That's just great," said Carl. "You should have told me that earlier, we could have left with the main audience, under cover. Now we're stuck here till the evening show."

"Don't worry," said Don. "I saw a trailer with a lot of cables earlier. Obviously there are landlines here. Give me a few moments on a keyboard with a terminal and we're home free."

"Dangerous," muttered Pappas. "If I tell my girlfriend about this kind of stuff, she is going to fire me on the spot."

"Don't tell her," said Don. "Look, we're going into that one.

It's empty."

"How can you tell?" Carl whispered. He felt very uncomfortable. Hanging around on the circus terrain hadn't bothered him until now. The scheme in his head didn't include this prolonged stay.

"I just saw someone come out and lock it," said Don.

"That proves nothing. It also means we have to unlock the lock," Carl muttered again.

"I know that trailer model. There's a hatch underneath and it's most likely not locked because most owners are unaware of it. It's for maintenance only."

"Sounds like a stupid model to me."

"Typical for these parts. People still leave their doors unlocked in these regions. Did you know that?"

"Wiseguy. All this knowledge can get you a second job at WCBN Radio, Don."

===

On his laptop screen, a thousand kilometers from the circus, Mach One looked at a seismographic report about the *Orianapocatl* volcano disturbances. Although the patterns in the graphic matched those of the previous one hundred years, the worn private eye didn't like what he was seeing.

Trouble is only trouble when you are sitting next to it, said one of his favorite mantras.

He didn't remember where he picked that one up. Probably from some old geezer in a distant time. Dictators and standup comedians had given the world many famous one-liners. Or perhaps he had made this one up himself, who knew?

The point of his thoughts was: if a volcano takes a hundred years to decide when to blow, he is going to do that when the bizz jockey is standing next to it. That's a law of nature.

But there was not a single official warning anywhere on the internet, because statistically it was a non-affair. The *Orianapocatl* was a sleeping volcano and no one was going to risk looking like a fool by warning for an imminent eruption. Not any more, after a hundred years.

He decided to text the bizz jockey anyhow.

Twenty-seven

This time, the trailer looked luxurious. Not from the outside; it had a plain facade of pale polyester, windows with the lamellae closed, only the driver's cabin exposing itself to the passer-by.

But on the inside, it was a small palace of leather upholstery, golden cranes, polished glass mirrors and high carpets.

Two clowns had escorted Hitomi to the trailer. They let her enter and then waited outside.

A few moments later, Mr. Angelos had arrived.

Another few moments later, they were relaxing in the luxury of the living room. The lights were comfortably dimmed, a nondescript brand of jazz music came from a hidden speaker and a fake fireplace produced an uninterrupted stream of identical flames. It came with the crackling sound of burning logs, much to Hitomi's amusement. It didn't take her long to notice that everything in this trailer was an imitation of the real thing.

Angelos noticed how she was looking around. "You like it?"

"This is the largest collection of imitations I have seen in my life," said Hitomi with a faint smile. "Is there anything genuine in this trailer?"

"Well done, Miss Sakamoto," cheered Angelos, clapping his hands fanatically. "You are one hell of an observer. Got it right the first time." He moved over on the couch, closer to Hitomi. "You know, most people are so impressed by the gold and the polishing and the carpets and the shining. It's very unusual for me to be with a woman who is not in the least impressed."

He poured two glasses of red wine and gave one to Hitomi.

"And that impresses me immensely, Miss Sakamoto," he said.

They touched glasses and then Hitomi burst into laughter, albeit a very short burst. "Oh, I apologize, Angel Angelo Angelos."

"What's so funny, Miss Hitomi?"

"Your clown's face," she said. "I can't help it. Your words don't go with the makeup and the hair and the hat."

Immediately, Angelos put down his glass and got up.

"You're not angry now, are you?"

"On the contrary, Miss Sakamoto. I am very grateful. I was about to kiss you and smear your face full of white and red makeup. A bloody shame, it would have been so embarrassing."

"Get rid of it then," said Hitomi. She touched his face, felt the stickiness of the make-up.

For a moment, Angelos hesitated. Then he walked away.

The trick, she knew, was going as far as possible without going too far. In the back of the trailer, she heard voices. Angelos was not alone back there — so that was good news.

She got up and walked in the direction that Angelos had

gone. There was a small corridor that ended in a large kitchen. On the other side was a wall-to-wall mirror. There was no doorknob or anything that resembled it, but the voices were coming from the other side of it. She couldn't understand a word of what was being said.

===

Right when Carl and Don were on their backs under the trailer, looking up, and Don was about to get to work to open the maintenance hatch, someone shouted at them.

"Hey, what are you guys doing under there? Come here right away!" They saw two legs and a face that was bent all the way down.

"Move," hissed Carl.

They crawled away from the intruder, who yelled after them. "You get back here!"

The feet started moving behind them, but it was a very long trailer, so Carl and Don were able to get out from under the house on wheels and disappear between the many other trailers here. They took a few turns and headed for the main tent.

"If he looks under the wagons," Carl said to Don, "he will be able to see where we're going."

"Too bad," said Don.

===

Hitomi pressed her ear against the mirror wall.

"He says there were two men crawling under the

communications trailer," a voice said. "He failed to capture them."

"What men?" said Angelos.

"Men in circus overalls," the other voice said. "It's unclear where they are right now."

"There are dozens of men in circus overalls," said Angelos in an unfriendly tone, something Hitomi had not heard him use yet.

"Whatever," said the other voice. "They made a run for it, no doubt about it. Why would they make a run for it if they were regular personnel?"

"Put the word out," said Angelos. "And put two of us on a search. Two guys who remember faces. There's something funny going..."

Then it was quiet.

Hitomi turned around and left the room. The high carpet muffled any noise she could possibly have made. She was a quiet walker, which helped.

Within moments after she sat down again, Angelos returned to the room. He looked around for a moment, his face — with the clown's makeup now removed — betraying suspicion.

"I'm sorry to say I have urgent matters to attend to," he said, putting a courteous face on all of a sudden. "I trust we can continue our little meeting at a later hour tonight?"

"You can count on it, Angel Angelos," said Hitomi. "I will leave you to it. But... now you have to go over the whole makeup process all over again before the show starts."

Angelos walked her to the exit and swung open the door for her, making a gracious gesture. "I am used to it," he said.

"By nature I am a man of many faces, as you undoubtedly know by now." He looked straight into her eyes, as if he was looking for a hidden response deep within.

"That would surprise me. You seem to me an honest man. A bit sad perhaps, like any clown. Should I be looking for clues?"

"Leave the looking for clues up to me, Miss Sakamoto. If there are any, you can be sure I will unearth them."

She nodded and stepped of the stairs into the cooled air of the early evening.

Behind her, the door was slammed shut.

What was that all about, Hitomi thought. What's with the clues game?

Angelos' words had indeed been full of hints. They worried her. It was time to catch up with the bizz jockey at one of the designated meeting points, because by the sound of it someone's cover had definitely been blown.

Twenty-eight

The main circus tent was semi-dark. It was only an hour until the evening's show commenced.

Under the grandstand Hitomi found Pappas and Wozniak.

"We were discovered," said Carl.

"So I've noticed," said Hitomi. "Any practical suggestions?"

"Yes," said the bizz jockey. "We need to hide for the moment, and then later, when the night gives us cover, we need to get back and upload our recordings. Once this is out in the open, we are covered by publicity."

"Can't we just walk out the main gate?" said Don. "If we abandon the overalls they won't think anything of it."

"Don Lech Wozniak," said Hitomi, "we'll assume that's your mouth talking independent from your brain. The audience won't arrive for at least forty minutes. Follow me. I will hide you in a place where they won't look."

===

Pjotr Aruin was Angelos' first man in the organization. They had worked together as boss and assistant for decades and when the transformation from the drugs business to the human trafficking began and the circus became their headquarters, he had assumed the role of lion tamer. He had been one many years ago, so deciding what to become had been a no-brainer. Rather than being a clown like most of the other staff members, he took on this macho part that impressed women, and practically everybody else. It also made hiding the refugees in the lions' cages a logical procedure.

Of course, Pjotr Aruin looked the part: a well-built man, who possessed everything he might need to become either a body builder, a body guard, a womanizer, a spokesperson, you name it. He had been all of that in some part of his long career and what had remained were the distinguished looks. Rough and scarred, but still graceful — not counting his menacing looks if he felt like looking that way.

Which happened more often every day.

Aruin had learned that it was not lions one should fear. Lions can be tamed. But a man like his boss Angel Angelo Angelos could not be restrained with a whip. And the man was sincerely pissed off tonight. With all the sweat running from his face while he was barking abuse at his gathering of armed clowns he would have a hard time putting on the clown's makeup on time for the show.

Besides Aruin there were some heavyweights in their clown outfits, standing around while Angelos walked through the group, spitting out insults and threats.

Then, all of a sudden, he stopped and changed his tone. "All right, forget it. I lost my temper. I'm all right now. No use getting upset over things that have already happened. If they are intruders, we are all in for the gallows. They could be some federal agency spying on us. The only thing we can do now, is watch the crowd. One thing: do not look for men in overalls. They will have ditched them by now. Don't try to pick people out of the audience as it will only cause more trouble and attract the wrong kind of attention. Just make sure that the most vulnerable part of our operation, our communications trailer, is guarded. Don't try to scare anyone off. If they're trying to break in? Let them. We'll take them on once they're inside."

Aruin walked to one of the men. He put a finger in his chest. "Shouting at them prematurely was your mistake. That was stupid. Now we don't know what they were up to plus you were unable to capture them."

The man did not reply. His clown's makeup was smeared and would scare any child right out of the tent.

"Go fix your face," said Aruin. "And next time, ask for backup before you do anything. Act dumb in public. What do you know?"

"What do I know?" said the man, fondling his rifle.

"I know what I said. I ask you again: what do you know?"

"I'm not sure, Mr. Aruin."

"Wrong. You know shit. You got that?"

"Yes, Sir."

"Anything goes down, you come to us and say: something's going down. You think you can handle that?"

"Yes."

"We'll see. Clowns can be shot from a cannon, you know."

Angelos laughed, finally. "It's a circus!" he yelled.

The mood loosened up a bit.

"That's better. Now go. Look dumb. Keep your clown's eyes open." He clapped hands and everybody understood. They walked out, only Aruin stayed put.

"What do you think, Aruin?"

"I think we're all becoming sissies. In the old days we wouldn't have tolerated this. One man would have been dead by now. We'd set an example."

"Oh come on Pjotr, that was a different business," said Angelos. "So we'll beef up, that's not important right now. Give me your assessment of the status quo if you please."

"It smells bad," said Aruin. "Even with one nostril closed." He put an index finger on his nose and pressed a nostril. It was the slightest gesture, but powerful nonetheless.

But Angelos didn't appreciate the subtlety. "What's with you tonight? A bout of poetic fever? Get out there and if it's as you say, well, shoot someone. I don't care. If this circus closes tonight, we must be sure this is behind us. Capiche?"

"We'll stamp each visitor's hand as they enter and take their picture at the same time. That way we have something to check when they leave," said Pjotr. "Someone tries to leave the premise without a stamp on his hand, we'll know." He checked his hair in one of the mirrors. Even at his advancing age he still had a young man's hairdo, albeit graying, and he kept it combed back meticulously. "Trust me, I have two guys who have dealt with that before. It's an emergency procedure and it's fully prepared. I'll have it operational in five minutes" — he checked his watch — "when the gates open."

As Pjotr Aruin left, self-confident as ever, Angelos rubbed his chin. He also checked his hair in the same mirror, but the sights didn't impress him the way Aruin had been impressed.

His phone beeped. He picked it up.

"Angelos... Yes... I'm not sure yet... I have an issue here... No... Here's what we'll do. Prepare another move on that Bizz Jockey... Because he seems like the right man to hit to get what we want. But postpone it for the time being. I'll know more in the morning. This either settles this evening, or we are in the shithouse."

He shut off the call and threw the phone on the table angrily. Perhaps Pjotr was right and this thing smelled worse than a wet dog's ass.

He closed one nostril with a finger.

Funny how a man like Aruin challenged the clichés: he kept on coming up with new stuff. He tried to detect a difference between smelling through one nostril and the other, and with two.

He felt like a clown.

Twenty-nine

So this was what being caged like an animal felt like. Sort of. Both Carl and Don were nauseated by the height, by knowing they could not escape, by breathing the circus breath of animals and people and food, by sitting like folded chairs in a dark corner.

The evening performance of the *Circus Oriano* was drawing to a close. The music and shouting of performers and audience and the roaring of animals pounded them from below. It was an exhausting situation.

Hitomi had smuggled the two men up the third tent pole. There were ladder sports attached to the outside of the pole, and that way it was possible to climb to the tent roof. Up there was a boardwalk that stretched from one end of the rectangular tent to the other. In the farthest corner from the entrance, an electricity booth was installed. Behind it was a little space left over and that's where Hitomi had brought them.

"No one comes here during the show," she had whispered. "Just sit here on the boardwalk until I come up again to get you down. Perfect hideaway for you guys."

"There's nothing perfect about any of this," growled Don to Pappas when there was a momentary lapse in volume from the circus arena and he could make himself heard. "My behind is turning to stone, my knees are fossilizing and my stomach is turning into an ammonia factory. I'm not sure if I can make it to the end of this show. I tell you she did this to punish me, Carl."

"Of course she did," said Pappas. "Now be quiet."

There were moments when they feared discovery. When a couple of trapeze artists stepped on the boardwalk and walked back and forth. Or when that guy came up and opened the electricity booth and did some hammering.

Then, all of a sudden, the show ended and the applause faded. Fifteen minutes later the tent was empty and semi-dark. When Hitomi showed up on the boardwalk in their dark corner another ten minutes later, Don cursed. But Carl noticed the tense look on his producer's face. Obviously, things were getting serious.

"Get out of this place," whispered Pappas to Hitomi as they climbed down. "Don and I must upload this recording first. If we get caught on the way out, at least we have brought the story to the outside world and we have something to bargain with."

"Carl Evangelos Pappas," hissed Hitomi in midair, "don't talk like a boy scout. We are in serious trouble. There are armed men looking for you and I am being scrutinized by the cartel boss."

But it was clear to each of them that there was no getting around this.

===

On the volcano's slope an old man walked with goats. It was a dry terrain for a man, but a grassy feast for a goat. There was enough to live on, and in the early night the grasses that sprouted from between the rocks cooled down. So in the moonlight the man sat on a rock and watched the animals as they moved about.

Way down in the deep he heard the sounds from the circus. He didn't like the circus. He thought about when he was a young boy and how they'd go to the circus all the time and how they were allowed on the premises on Saturday afternoons to feed the horses and play soccer with some of the trapeze artists or even go into the lion's cage with the trainer. They'd be scared to death for a few moments and were sent home with ice cream.

Nowadays, new people had taken over the circus management and some of them were seen armed every now and then and the place was closed like a prison. Strange stories were told.

No, they weren't going to find him in the circus no more. But while he thought that again and again, he heard a rumbling under his feet. His dog started barking and then there was the rushing of earth and bleating and several of the dark goat shades disappeared into the earth. Hot steam emerged, lit by the moon and moving around as if it were attacking the dog.

Too bad, he thought. Darned goats, that's going to cost me.

The rumbling had stopped again, but he remembered how his grandfather had told him about how his great-great-grandfather had told him about the last eruption and how it had destroyed the livelihood of farmers for miles around, and killed several of them and how that also meant an end to a farmer's financial worries.

Perhaps it was just as well.

===

It is time to call a friend of mine, thought Mach One at that very moment. He was still looking at the computer screen, the only light in his derelict hotel room, and didn't like what he was seeing.

This volcano is no longer asleep, he thought as he grabbed one of his anonymous cell phones.

===

It took the hatch an eternity to open. By the time Don succeeded, Carl's arm was numb from holding up the tiny pocket light. They had at least agreed not to do any talking as long as the operation was going on, so that saved them both a lot of complaining. The hatch fell on Don's face, but he didn't say anything. Carl lit his sound engineer's face, but there was no blood or nothing, so they were good to go.

They climbed into the trailer and found themselves in a storage room. Without wasting any more time, they opened the storage room door and entered the small corridor that led them to the other rooms. Apparently, Don knew where to find the equipment that would bring them online.

Thirty

The whole settirg was an exact copy of that afternoon.

The shining room with leather upholstery and girandoles and high carpets and strange imitations of famous soul music, some incense and two glasses of fine wine.

Angel Angelo Angelos on the leather couch extremely close to Hitomi Sakamoto.

They had just touched glasses and took a sip.

She had tried to get away before Angelos invited her to his trailer once again, but failed. It had been the wrong time to raise suspicions by refusing his invitation. Anyway, she decided she had a more urgent reason to accept: by being close to Angelos she would be the first to notice if the bizz jockey and his sound engineer got into trouble.

Besides, Angelos was a charming man, especially now that his clown's makeup and suit had been removed and he was dressed like a ladies' man. That quieted her inner voice, the one that was going on about how irresponsible all of this was and how they were going to have to abandon this type of investigation in the near future. She could relax quite easily. It wasn't the drink, it was the soft and deep voice of Angelos, and the smooth lines that were flowing from him about how attractive she was, and how he felt she was like a beautiful alien in his strange land, and how well built she was and yet so thin and fragile...

"You are a muscle miracle," he whispered as they were getting closer and closer.

Such a mature man, Hitomi thought.

All the men in her daily life regarded her as a threat to their masculinity, and perhaps worse. In the city, men liked independent women for work and perhaps some dating or dancing, but they also felt you didn't have to take any romantic initiative. An independent woman can take the initiative herself, can't she? Why whisper romantic secrets into her ear? Utterly pointless — so Hitomi led a life virtually deprived of that imaginary fireplace of the heart. To be honest: she hardly ever thought about it because she was used to it. It was what an independent woman's life in the city was about.

But it made her an easy target when she was not in her daily work environment, pulling virtually everybody's string. She was vaguely aware of this strange effect, but after all the stress of infiltrating the circus she felt comfortable relaxing for a moment. She was here to observe only, anyway.

"Miss Sakamoto," said Angelos, while he reached around her and touched her ponytail, "I am beginning to believe you are here for a higher reason than merely as earthly as work. Before I start believing you are heaven sent for my personal happiness, tell me: why are you here, really? Is it because you have an insatiable appetite for danger?"

"I was born into danger," whispered Hitomi as she moved

closer. "I have tried to shed it, but I accept it is always with me. You know how that feels, don't you, Angel Angelo Angelos?"

His nostrils shivered as he grabbed her ponytail, gentle but firm.

===

Aruin walked by the communications trailer to check things out. He did so very quietly, approaching in the shadows of the evening, giving the clown with the rifle all the stimuli for a heart attack. The man cocked his rifle and entered attack mode, only to realize that it was one of his bosses who had materialized out of thin air.

"Please don't do that, Mr. Aruin," said the clown, once he had regained his self-control. Without the circus lights, in the dark evening his face looked like it was scarred, the skin pale and the mouth ruined. "People are very jumpy. We don't want to start shooting at one another."

"Be quiet," whispered Aruin. "Why aren't you inside the trailer?" He looked around him.

"This is the only door," said the clown.

In the distance, the volcano rumbled. The men turned and looked at its moonlit peak in the distance.

"That thing is beginning to give everybody the creeps."

"You mean it is giving *you* the creeps," said Aruin sarcastically. "If it blows, it blows and our problems will be over. Right now, the only thing to fear is the possibility of an outside infiltration of our operation. Standing outside a door is not going to lure anybody into a trap. So go inside, leave the door unlocked and give them a chance to run into you unexpected. Come one, I'll go in with you and see that you're set up. I'll also call two more guys. This is ridiculous. I can't believe it."

===

"I can't believe they leave their communications trailer unattended like this," whispered Carl. "I mean, a man outside at the door, that's a laugh. Makes me feel confident we can pull this off. Are you coming along with that uploading?"

"Yes," said Don. "It's done. You want to add anything to the recordings? Mike's open. Now we're here, might as well add a little extra narrative."

"I wouldn't do that if I were you," a voice hollered behind them. "Because anything you say can kill you."

A gentleman and a clown stood in the doorway, pointing a gun and an automatic rifle at them.

"Smile," said Carl Pappas. "You're on live radio."

===

In the middle of a kiss that had a momentary eternity in it, Angelos tightened his grip on Hitomi's ponytail and jerked it. "Why are you here, bitch?" he yelled.

Thirty-one

Hitomi faced the gun while Angelos talked into his cell phone. Her head hurt from the jerking at her hair.

"A whole police squadron? When? A half hour? OK, listen... NO! Take them to the lions' truck, I'm on my way there now. Spread the word that everyone hides weapons and that it is business as usual. Plan 7 is now operational, on the double!"

He put the phone away. "Listen, little lady, I have no idea who you people are, but I can assure you that I will find out before you die!"

Then he grabbed her elbow and pushed her out the door, down the steps into the night air. In the distance, the volcano coughed and they both stopped walking for a moment to look up in amazement.

"Is that.... smoke?" said Angelos.

"Yeah," said Hitomi. "Romantic, isn't it? A drink, a night walk, a smoking volcano..."

"Shut up," growled Angelos.

He pushed her forward through the jungle of trailers and trucks. But he couldn't help looking up at the mountain every time it became visible between the mobile homes. "That can't be good."

The terrain seemed to be empty of regular circus personnel. Perhaps they had smelled the dangers that were about to erupt and had vanished into their mobile homes. But more and more armed clowns joined them on the way and when they finally got to the lions' truck, there were at least a dozen of Angelos' army.

"I can't believe this," he said angrily, holding on to Hitomi. "Everybody spread out. Hide your guns. Go watch TV in your trailer. Go to the bath trailer. But remember: look busy. The police are coming. Go. Make sure you are acting according to emergency plan 7."

The order was followed instantly. Even Aruin disappeared in the darkness between the trailers and trucks, leaving Carl Pappas and Don Wozniak with Hitomi and Angelos.

"We'll deal with you clowns later," said Angelos. "You can rest assured. For now, you lady and you two gentlemen will kindly mount this truck."

They climbed the stairs and walked into the lion's trailer.

"Weren't you a clown too?" asked Pappas. "I thought I saw you getting a pie in the face."

"Actually, no. I was the one who did the throwing," said Angelos. "Now shut up and move forward to the cage in the middle."

The animals were restless, no doubt from the volcano's rumbling in the distance. They seemed to ignore the visitors as they walked up and down their cages.

"Stand still," ordered Angelos. From a hook on the wall he took a whip and opened the door to the center cage. He swung it open with force and cracked the whip simultaneously. The lion backed off. "Everybody come in."

His gun had been pointing at the three of them all the time. There was little else for them to do but enter the cage.

"In the middle, swipe the hay aside and open up the hatch," barked Angelos. "And muy rapidamenta if you please."

"Nice international tongue you got there," said Carl, as he bent over the hatch with Don and opened up the black hole underneath.

There was an immense bang in the air, like an exploding bomb in the distance, followed by a hollering thunder that seemed to be coming from everywhere.

"The volcano." yelled Hitomi.

Before Angelos had regained his focus, taking it back from the volcano's rumbling to the cage, the lion was all over him.

Thirty-two

The border was colored in the red of blood. The light of the moon shone down on a bank of foggy smoke hanging over the mountains, and from below a strange glow from the volcano's peak reflected downward as if some giant was pouring red ink into the landscape.

A series of police cars and army vehicles, dozens of them, was racing across a dusty road, slaloming around hole after hole, their sirens drowned in the angry thundering of the *Orianapocatl*. Above them, three helicopters hovered along, their sound also suffocated. In the red light, they looked like giant insects, each with one shining red eye.

But before they reached the circus compound gate, the helicopters hesitated and stopped. For a moment they circled around, then turned in an orderly fashion and rushed away again, spraying dust in the air.

The line of cars stopped in front of the gate, their sirens blaring, their lights fighting the red glow from above. Police and soldiers jumped out to check whether the gate was really shut and there were no people on the other side. Then they beckoned an army truck. It raced towards the gate and crash right through it. Police officers and soldiers ran onto the circus compound, starting to search people, ask for their IDs, while an older officer climbed on the truck and started speaking through a megaphone. Only shards of his speech could be heard through the volcano's anger.

"This is a police search as well as an evacuation... have reason to believe that the volcano... to go off... show your ID when asked and then get in your vehicles to move away from this area..."

The ensuing chaos was unfathomable. Hundreds of people, already on the thresholds of their mobile homes or standing in the open air, looking at the volcano, started to run in all directions. Some were showing their IDs to officers, some were climbing into the cabins of their trailers or mobile homes, blowing horns to warn the vehicles in front of them to move out of the way.

None of the regular circus personnel had gone to the back lot of the compound. That remote area had been the domain of the Angelos cartel for over a year and no one wanted to mingle in their affairs — certainly not at night. So the armed clowns and men in overalls now had the space all to themselves. In spite of the arrival of the police force, they all felt kind of lucky because three helium balloons had just been filled and erected. All of them had climbed aboard and were waiting for the sign to cut the cables and take off. Within minutes, the invaders would be there, so Aruin made it to the lions' trailer as fast as he could; it was the last chance to find Angelos or he would have to give him up.

He ran into the three people Angelos had been meaning to

lock up: the trapeze woman and the two burglars.

"Hold it right there," shouted Aruin. "Where is Angelos?"

Only now did he notice the woman's sad look.

"Listen," said one of the men, "he made a mistake in there. We couldn't help him. You're lucky the lion didn't escape."

"What!" shouted Aruin again. Confusion took him over as he jumped the steps and landed in the trailer's interior. He walked slowly to the center of the truck, his gun pointed in front of him with both hands, trying to distinguish one thing from the other in the dim light. He saw the shades of lions move back and forth and since he couldn't see if they were locked up properly, his heart started pounding like crazy and sweat started to flow from him like lava from an active volcano.

Then he saw the blood and the smeared mouth of the lion in the center cage and the shadow on the floor.

"Angelos..." whispered Aruin.

Then his consciousness returned in full power, made him turn and run out of that dreadful place. He left a whole life behind him.

===

Trying to convince the police officers took too much time. Carl, Hitomi and Don had run from the lion's truck to the front of the circus compound, only to be held at gunpoint, and be questioned and shouted at. They simply barked back, all three of them, but it was the voice of Hitomi Sakamoto that did the trick. Screaming men were business as usual, but the words this woman was speaking and the way she spit them out put a stop to the inquisition. Once they had summoned the police chief, things were cleared instantly.

"I have been informed of your covert operation, Mr. Pappas," he said. "Please tell me what you know."

"Forget that," yelled Carl, as he turned and started running again. "Come with me and hurry, they're about to escape."

But already, as they ran, the balloons could be seen as they shot into the red sky. Their speed was beyond recognition. Almost by default, one expects balloons to rise slowly and gracefully — but these three seemed to have been catapulted into the air. The clowns looked down from the baskets like crazy dolls, armed to the teeth and grinning insane smiles.

"Hold your fire!" yelled the commanding officer in his megaphone. "I repeat: hold your fire."

They stopped right where the cut cables of the balloons laid on the ground.

"If we should fire, they'd fall to their deaths," said the commander. "That gets us nowhere. We'll focus on the evacuation."

They turned and started running back to the gate, where the first vehicles were already driving through, while behind them the three helium balloons — now at a safe distance from the police and army — were being sucked towards the red cloud hovering over the volcano.

Thirty-three

It is not easy to escape the wrath of a volcano. If you are on the slopes, it is unlikely that you can run fast and far enough to stay out of the way of the pyroclastic cloud. While such hot gas and rock can travel at an astonishing seven hundred kilometers per hour, it's just as lethal at a lower velocity. Fortunately, the Orianapocatl was at the other side of the border than where the circus lay. Too far away to be a real threat to the bizz jockey and his team. Or all the other refugees for that matter: the police, the soldiers, the circus personnel and their livestock.

They took the precaution, led by the military vehicles, to drive at least fifteen kilometers until they stopped. The sky was covered in a dark gray-red ocean of clouds, and an intimidating thunder continued to come down from it.

Half a mile of vehicles stood by the side of the road, its passengers standing around looking at what could be seen of the volcano in the distance. Its slopes were almost entirely shrouded in dark gray clouds.

"No man deserves to die like that," said Hitomi to her boss, the bizz jockey.

They stood leaning against a car. A few meters away, Don Wozniak was chatting with soldiers about radio technology, trying to find out if they were using any kind of new equipment. He was showing them his mobile recording device, a sure way of getting their attention and lowering their professional defenses.

"No," said Carl, his thoughts miles away. And then, confused: "Do you mean the clowns in the balloons? Them flying right into the volcano?"

"No," snapped Hitomi. "For all I know they made it and escaped. No, I mean Angel Angelo Angelos. To be attacked by a lion. Such a violent death. He was... He had grace."

Carl knew better than to put a finger on the real talents of Angelos. This was not the right time to preach about the violent rule of the Angelos cartel in their cocaine days. Nor about the abuse of vulnerable refugees or the extortion of money and sexual favors from them. So he just thought of something nice to say, when all of a sudden his mouth fell open.

"Don't say it, Carl Evangelos Pappas," said Hitomi. "Because I don't want to hear it."

"No... I mean, look!"

A light flashed in the sky. Short after, the sound of a bang. An army of flames exploded right under the clouds; fiery soldiers flaring around each other, embracing, letting go, trying to escape upwards.

"You gotta be joking!" yelled Carl.

Two more balloons, close to their exploded teammate, tried to get away from the scene, get away from the heat of the clouds, but they were too late. In a last attempt they bumped into each other and then exploded in one giant burst. Even the baskets disappeared in the flames.

"These guys are absolute beginners," said Don, as he joined Carl and Hitomi again.

They watched some debris as it whirled down towards the ground.

"They're clowns, Don," said Carl. "What did you expect? Whatever they do is supposed to go wrong."

"We can joke about it, but it's only one cartel that's been dismantled," said Carl, angry all of a sudden. "It's just lots of dead people behind us and a road to freedom cut off for many to come. What have we achieved, really?"

Hitomi turned and pressed her index finger into Carl's chest. "You are the bizz jockey. You are going to shout abuse across international radio. You are going to influence lawmakers by explaining the powers that be. A lot of people are making money on refugees and that can only be stopped if crossing borders is no longer illegal. So get on it, Pappas."

She turned and walked away.

"That's an opinion, Sakamoto!" yelled the bizz jockey.

Don giggled. "I love her when she's angry."

Carl walked after her.

"You think she may actually hit us one day?" Don yelled after his boss. And then, to himself: "I may have to expand my insurance policy first."

Thirty-four

"We are grateful for the actions of the bizz jockey," said Ramon Rodriguez. "I humble myself in the presence of a man who faced cartel clowns, lions and volcanoes to defend refugees like my family and me."

Applause sounded from the studio table. In the semi-darkness, Carl Pappas, the bizz jockey, was surrounded by Ramon, his wife Larissa, his children Carolina, Raoul and Emmeline, and Secretary of Internal Affairs Anthony Plummer. From behind one of the studios windows, his producer Hitomi Sakamoto looked on with a stern look on her face. While seated next to her, Don Wozniak watched his console in utter relaxation. For him, the challenge of a noisy audience was a welcome change from routine.

"Grand as that may be," continued Rodriguez, "and free as we may be from the claws of these smugglers, it saddens me to think about all the people who are still on the other side of the border. All the families who will find the street gangs on their doorstep one of these days, being forced to hand over their daughters. All the shop owners who are being robbed of their sales. All the children and adults who must cross the streets to school or work every day and risk the bullet. It is a life without a future, and whether we like it or not, it is traffic cartels like that of The Clown that provides them with an escape route."

Again, there was an applause.

"Governments do nothing while cartels help us!" shouted Rodriguez through the noise. "Bad, expensive help, but still."

When the applause had faded, Carl Pappas said: "You are hitting the nail on the head, my dear Ramon. That's why I'm happy to introduce you to your other guest at the table, Mr. Anthony Plummer, Secretary of Internal Affairs. He suffered a terrible ordeal starting at this very table only because he believed in helping the immigrants. He was kidnapped right here in this very studio by a branch of Angelos' cartel called the Immigration Block. Without a head, their organization will probably wither away. Welcome Anthony. Last thing I remember is you wanted to withdraw from public office. So now you're back. That's quite a turnaround in little more than a week. What made you change your mind?"

There was a silence.

Hitomi held her breath, for none of this had been rehearsed and the Secretary had been less than talkative before the show. He had only seemed interested in security measures. Had the building been properly secured? Had all entrances to the studio floor, be it doors, elevators, stairs, windows and ventilation shafts been guarded?

But his security obsession seemed to have faded as he started talking.

"It was your radio show about what you found on the border, Mr. Pappas. The transporting of people in helium balloons in the night. Hiding them under the floorboards of a lion cage. The violence of the cartel people, the guns, the threats, the abuse. I thought, well, I'm safe here now. Let's proceed and look at the whole immigration issue with new eyes. Borders are supposed to be a hurdle against criminals and illegal trade, but they've also become hurdles for ordinary people."

Another applause sounded, by now beginning to irritate the producer. 'Can they listen for more than one minute without clapping hands?" she sighed.

"It's enthusiasm, Hitomi," said Don, opening a can of soda. "You should try some."

"Now that it's public knowledge that some groups are trying to obstruct an honest debate about immigration, it will be easier to deal with it. Now everybody knows the forces we are up against. It is not just about criminals, it is about a wrongful influencing of public opinion. Mr. Rodriguez has made it quite clear that more than anything else he wants to return to his country to help clean it up and make it better. Well, I second that motion. We need to stabilize both our own nation as well as the nation all these people are running away from. So to take the first step, I've sent off a group of experts to Mr. Rodriguez' nation and evaluate whatever it takes to turn things around. We need to elevate our neighbors to a point where running away is no longer necessary and cartel crimes can vanish. If illegal immigration is an economic problem, then let's deal with it in an economic way," said Plummer, again drowned in applause. This time, Don Wozniak joined, but as he was still holding his soda, Hitomi got understandably put-off.

"Don Lech Wozniak, knock that off at once! The Boardroom is not a place for applause. It sounds cheap. Why don't you do your job and try to filter out at least some of this pointless clapping."

"OK," said Don, putting his soda can away.

He stood up and hugged Hitomi before she could step back. "It's hard if there's so much applause and none of it is meant for you. I'm really sorry no one is clapping for you."

The producer stood there, frozen, until he let go and sat down again.

"If you do that again," said Hitomi, "there will be a lot more clapping. On you."

***

Request from the author

Thank you for reading this Radio Detective adventure. I hope you enjoyed it and will be willing to write a review on the online platform of your choice. Making that extra effort is greatly appreciated by other readers... and of course by me. Thank you.

I hope you and I stay connected through Twitter, Facebook, Google+, Pinterest or my free email newsletter. I'll make sure you'll stay tuned.

Have a good evening/night/day!

M.H. Vesseur

Twitter @MHVesseur

Facebook www.facebook.com/MHVesseur

Subscribe to M.H. Vesseur's mailing list on www.mhvesseur.com

About the author

M.H. Vesseur has written many short stories for literary magazines in The Netherlands, Belgium, Canada and the U.S.A. He was awarded for the best debut with his first story. In his radio detective series about Carl Pappas he has now written and published the seven short crime novels *CEO Groupie*, *Die Rich*, *Tax Me If You Can*, *Acid Asset*, *Nosedive*, *Power Play* and *Blood Border*. The radio detective's producer Hitomi Sakamoto now stars in her own series, which begins with *North*. M.H. Vesseur also published the novel *Lemniscate*, a collection of literary short stories called *Allusions* and his outlook on the super economy *Burning Neil Armstrong*. M.H. Vesseur is an awarded advertising copywriter. He lives in the forests of The Netherlands.

www.mhvesseur.com

Novels and ebooks by M.H. Vesseur

More information on:
www.mhvesseur.com/publications

Allusions (short story collection)
North (The Hitomi Files: 1)
Blood Border (a Radio Detective novel)
Power Play (a Radio Detective novel)
Nosedive (a Radio Detective novel)
Acid Asset (a Radio Detective novel)
Tax Me If You Can (a Radio Detective novel)
Die Rich (a Radio Detective novel)
CEO Groupie (a Radio Detective novel)
Beloved Stalker
Babyface Junkie
In Snuff Park
Sketches Of A Worldwide Christo And Jeanne-Claude
Narcissist Guru
Territory Game

Short stories by M.H. Vesseur

ALLUSIONS

Glimpses of tomorrow await you in this collection. The ultimate amusement park will offer you death. Everlasting youth will take you to the point of no return. The artificial landscape will fill you with joy if it doesn't scare the living daylights out of you. The Narcissist Guru will show you your many selves. There is the ultimate work of art that will change the planet and the old vaudeville star who is still being stalked. And finally, the coming of the super economy will haunt your dreams. This collection contains the short stories • In Snuff Park • Babyface Junkie • Narcissist Guru • Sketches of a Worldwide Christo and Jeanne-Claude • Territory Game • Beloved Stalker • Burning Neil Armstrong.

Available in The Hitomi Files by M.H. Vesseur

NORTH

Man should fear only one enemy

The only enemy who has the capacity to remove all of mankind from the earth, is the virus. Imagine the worst of them all, a true 21st century killer. It lies dormant in the remote laboratory of a pharmaceutical giant whose hopes of making billions off a vaccine somewhere in the future throw a dark shadow ahead. Then Hitomi Sakamoto, the hard boiled radio producer who's on a rough vacation in the wild nature of the north, stumbles upon this dark secret. She is drawn into a final battle between ruthless scientists, a greedy corporation, desperate but dangerous environmental activists, a cold-hearted assassin and... a manmade virus that longs to escape.

Hitomi Sakamoto first appeared in the Radio Detective novels by

M.H. Vesseur. Immediately popular for her iron work ethics and razorsharp tongue, Hitomi outgrew her boss (radio detective Carl Pappas) and now steps out of his shadow, into her very own adventure.

Available in the radio detective series by M.H. Vesseur

CEO GROUPIE - A radio detective novel

One night three live guests join Carl Pappas on his radio show The Boardroom: two CEOs and a woman who calls herself: "the CEO Groupie". When the mysterious woman reveals the existence of a secret call girl organization for CEOs and subsequently disappears a couple of days later, the bizz jockey engages on a search. What happened to the CEO Groupie and what are the other two guests up to? Together with his radio team — his producer Hitomi Sakamoto and his sound engineer Don Wozniak — Carl Pappas sets out to deal with this.

Available in the radio detective series by M.H. Vesseur

DIE RICH - A radio detective novel

Carl Pappas, the bizz jockey, goes on the air again. His radio show "The Boardroom" is both loved and feared by the global business community. He has a sharp eye for business news and the big mouth of a talk radio host. This time around he has some very wealthy guests joining him on his show: two billionaire entrepeneurs and their future successors, who also happen to be their sons. Of course it doesn't take the bizz jockey a very long time to upset some of his guests and his audience — and that same night the bizz jockey finds himself heading into dangerous waters, in the hands of some very angry rich people. His team — producer Hitomi Sakamoto and sound engineer Don Wozniak — is forced to go out and rescue their reckless boss. And then there are the rich kids they have to deal with...

Available in the radio detective series by M.H. Vesseur

TAX ME IF YOU CAN - A radio detective novel

Carl Pappas, the bizz jockey, is cooking up a real shocker: during a live broadcast of his popular business talk radio show "The Boardroom" he plans to reveal secrets about tax dodging practices around the globe. In the middle of the preparations he and his producer Hitomi Sakamoto face unexpected trouble. Who is trying to shut the Bizz Jockey up in this quiet country under the tropical sun? Is it the local military junta? Is it the business community? Or is the sun finally getting to Carl Pappas' head?

Available in the radio detective series by M.H. Vesseur

ACID ASSET - A radio detective novel

Carl Pappas, the bizz jockey, is feeling good about the prospects of environment-friendly plastics he's discussing on his radio show "The Boardroom". But as he soon finds out there's something not right with the company behind it. Can the bizz jockey protect a lonely scientist against the schemes of a large corporation that smells money? Or will he be unable to stop a revolutionary asset from becoming really acidic? Buckle up for a race against arsonists, corporate crime, dogs, bullets and a dangerous industrial zone in the middle of a blizzard, softened only by some real team spirit.

Also available in the radio detective series

NOSEDIVE - A radio detective novel

When a large corporation is struck by a cripling strike among its workers and an apparent terrorist attack on its factory, bizz jockey Carl Pappas steps forward to offer his public support. But as he soon finds out, there's more to the picture than meets the eye. Why is the owner hiding in her large mansion? What happened in her youth that is threatening her after all these years? It's a job for the radio detective — and this time around his boss gives an unexpected hand.

Available in the radio detective series by M.H. Vesseur

POWER PLAY - A radio detective novel

The death of an environmental activist brings bizz jockey and unofficial "radio detective" Carl Pappas to the quiet island of Islasol. Everything seems to be OK with the local National Park and the wind turbine park in the heart of it.

But Carl and his team soon find out you can't take anything on face value. Below the surface of an environment friendly enterprise lies a darker secret. It's time for the radio detective to unravel the local secrets of wind energy, assisted by his producer Hitomi and a new, unlikely ally.

<<<<>>>>

www.ingramcontent.com/pod-product-compliance
Lightning Source LLC
Chambersburg PA
CBHW030302130626
46549CB00002B/661